"I bet you were a very naughty school-boy," Sandy teased as they watched the rowdy children run away.

Never breaking her gaze, Alex nodded in serious agreement. "Very naughty."

Mesmerized by his low voice and the sparkling blue of his eyes, she whispered back, "How naughty?"

"This naughty," he murmured. Cupping her chin in his fingers, he brushed his lips against hers, then pulled back. His kiss was the last thing she'd expected, but her response surprised her more. "That's not so naughty."

Without a word, he slipped his arm around her and drew her close for another try. He began the kiss, like the first, with a passing brush at her lips, but the sensation of his touch as he began nipping at her mouth spilled through her like liquid sunshine, and soon her mouth tingled for the attention he was lavishing on its corners. He'd been polite, helpful, even funny up to now, but this was a different Alex Stoner. Passionate. Inviting. Arousing. And aroused. She groaned with the overwhelming pleasure he was giving her. No one had ever kissed her like this, and she'd never imagined a kiss could be so wonderful. . . .

WHAT ARE *LOVESWEPT* ROMANCES?

They are stories of true romance and touching emotion. We believe those two very important ingredients are constants in our highly sensual and very believable stories in the *LOVESWEPT* line. Our goal is to give you, the reader, stories of consistently high quality that may sometimes make you laugh, sometimes make you cry, but are always fresh and creative and contain many delightful surprises within their pages.

Most romance fans read an enormous number of books. Those they truly love, they keep. Others may be traded with friends and soon forgotten. We hope that each *LOVESWEPT* romance will be a treasure—a "keeper." We will always try to publish

*LOVE STORIES YOU'LL NEVER FORGET
BY AUTHORS YOU'LL ALWAYS REMEMBER*

The Editors

Loveswept® 606

Susan Connell
Some Kind of Wonderful

BANTAM BOOKS
NEW YORK · TORONTO · LONDON · SYDNEY · AUCKLAND

SOME KIND OF WONDERFUL

A Bantam Book / April 1993

If you would be interested in receiving protective vinyl
covers for your Loveswept books, please write to this address
for information:

Loveswept
Bantam Books
P.O. Box 985
Hicksville, NY 11802

ISBN 0-553-44373-9

Published simultaneously in the United States and Canada

Bantam Books are published by Bantam Books, a division of
Bantam Doubleday Dell Publishing Group, Inc. Its trademark,
consisting of the words "Bantam Books" and the portrayal of
a rooster, is Registered in U.S. Patent and Trademark Office
and in other countries. Marca Registrada. Bantam Books, 666
Fifth Avenue, New York, New York 10103.

PRINTED IN THE UNITED STATES OF AMERICA

OPM   0 9 8 7 6 5 4 3 2 1

Jim—for that wonderful time in Greece.

One

Alex Stoner could think of several reasons why he should return to his office, but only one to linger over his lunch in the Plaka. And she wasn't even his type. He checked his watch, then shook his head as laughter rumbled in his chest. Was he crazy? He'd spent almost two hours trying to make eye contact with a tourist—who was so busy shopping for souvenirs she hadn't noticed him. He smiled. Ah, but what a tourist. Those long legs, that willowy figure, and the face of an angel . . .

"Get a grip, Stoner," he said to himself, drumming his fingers on the table. This was his last full day in Athens before he flew out to his island retreat. Plenty of work was waiting back at Stoner Exports, plus that mysterious three-fifteen appointment. He rolled his eyes as more tasks came to mind. He hadn't packed, and somehow he was going to have to fit in a rug-factory inspection. And he still had work to do on the upcoming meeting with the Grimaldi brothers.

He began reaching for his sunglasses, then hesitated. The trees were shading him from the late May sun, his street table offered an excellent view of the

Acropolis, and another Athens siesta was about to begin. More important, he told himself as he settled back in his chair, it didn't hurt to look.

"She's not your type, Alex."

Alex glanced sideways at the *taverna* owner, groaning just loud enough for Dimitri to hear and smile.

"You know me too well, Dimitri, but I passed up the honey cakes today, and I ought to have something sweet." He looked down the narrow street, searching for the slender brunette.

"You should be at home sampling the sweets of a wife, my friend. Making sons." Presenting the check, Dimitri demanded as only an old friend could, "What happened to the French girl?"

Alex stood, pulled several bills from his pocket, and placed them on the table. "She left me."

"I know she left you. But *why?*"

Alex's gaze had strayed back to the little shop blaring bouzouki music. He checked his watch again. The brunette had gone in there fifteen minutes ago. "If you must know," he murmured absently, "because I wouldn't take her to Zephyros with me."

Dimitri patted his own shirtsleeves, then laughed loudly, causing several pedestrians to turn and look their way. "She demanded a piece of your soul, and you wouldn't share it," he said.

Again, a knowing look passed between the two men. Alex had fallen in love with the uncomplicated lifestyle on Zephyros years ago. Although he could never quite explain it to himself, he'd made it a point never to mix his city life with his island life. Keeping his business clients away was easy enough. The hard part was keeping a lover from finding out about Zephyros. Dimitri offered him a scolding look, then retreated into the *taverna.* Alex retrained his eyes on the pedestrian-filled street.

For seven years he'd lived and worked in Athens. Seven years and he couldn't remember the last time he'd stretched a nonbusiness lunch to three o'clock. He ran his fingers through his straight blond hair and sat back down. Hadn't he read that life ran in seven-year cycles? An amusing thought, but he doubted it. Of course, if he were approaching a momentous change, it wouldn't hinge on eye contact with a pretty stranger.

With Dimitri's distracting conversation he'd lost sight of her. Where had she gone? He lit a cigarette, then stubbed it out after two puffs. He was quitting. It was just a matter of time.

Where was that brunette, and why had she made such an impression? Perhaps it was her youthful energy that had captured his attention, or the casual manner in which she flipped back her shimmering curtain of hair. The way she moved in her short denim skirt, pink sweater, and pink leather flats reminded him of girls from his college days. He thought about that for a moment. The appeal of a college girl to his thirty-three-year old self seemed vaguely perverse, or worse, reeking of sentimentality.

He felt his eyebrows lift with that last revelation, because if Alex Stoner knew anything about himself, he knew he wasn't a sentimental fool. Not the way some men were. Still, there was something warmly satisfying about the brunette. From a distance, he could handle "warmly satisfying."

After several minutes his waiting was rewarded. She stood in the middle of the street counting her money, in view of every pickpocket in the popular shopping district. She wet her lips, then rested the tip of her tongue in the corner of her mouth as she mentally calculated. He shook his head in masculine appreciation. She was probably being overcharged by every merchant in the Plaka. Shifting several packages, she began walking in his direction. With unnamed relief, Alex reassessed her age as late twenties. She was definitely alone, and by the looks of it, doing her best to bring the art of souvenir shopping to new heights.

Large gold earrings danced against her jaw and in and out of the long curves of her hair. He leaned forward in his chair. Her eyes were the color of root beer, and they were eagerly drinking in her surroundings.

Then it happened.

Alex caught her gaze and held it. She smiled warmly. He returned the smile quickly and reached for another cigarette. What the hell had he expected? A flirty little wink, an open invitation to join her, or even a quick roll of her eyes to discourage him? Any of that wouldn't have surprised him, but that smile . . . that warm and open smile. He lit the cigarette and drew in deeply. A familiar loneliness resonated painfully within him. He didn't like stirring up those feelings, and avoided them whenever they started emerging. Besides, he was getting too old for this kind of torture.

Repositioning her packages again, she tossed her hair away from one eye and checked her watch. Without another glance, she hurried into a narrow alleyway.

"A guileless one," announced Dimitri from the doorway. He pulled a cloth from the glass he was polishing and shook the twisted material at Alex. "You always manage to pass them up, but if you hurry—"

"Always," Alex confirmed, picking up his cigarettes. He slipped them in his shirt pocket, gave his friend a mock salute, and began his walk back to his office.

With her arms wrapped firmly around the carton, Sandy Patterson scurried up the steps of the office building and elbowed open the glass doors marked Stoner Exports. Passing the display of flokati and hand-woven rugs, she made her way down the marble hall, praying that she hadn't missed Alex Stoner.

His secretary had been polite but firm when she'd telephoned yesterday. "Mr. Stoner's calendar is completely filled, but I'll try to fit you in at three-fifteen tomorrow. Please be on time. He's going on a trip and won't be back for several weeks."

Setting the carton on the first desk she came to, Sandy smoothed the sides of her short denim skirt, pushed up the sleeves of her sweater, and gave in to the first sign of tension since she'd arrived in Greece yesterday. She inhaled, looked around the large reception area, then exhaled sharply. No doubt about it. She was late, and every desk in the reception area was empty. Damn. Her mandatory gift shopping was just about done, and she wanted this chore out of the way too. Then she could get on with her own plans. For once free of duties, obligations, and other people's expectations, she was going to spend the summer painting whatever she felt like painting. When her advanced art classes began in the autumn, she was going to be thoroughly inspired by this trip. Life was suddenly exciting again, and its possibilities for happiness were endless. She felt ready for anything—except rescheduling this meeting with Alex Stoner.

Reaching into her shoulder bag, she pulled out the business card. Except for a bent corner, the card was in the same crisp condition as when she'd received it two years ago. The small white card with the bright blue lettering had been tucked in with Alex Stoner's letter of condolence over her husband's death. She rubbed her thumb over the name as she thought about her late husband. Jackson had always insisted on black ink for his cards and stationery.

"Black is not only appropriate, Sandy, it's the perfect statement of sincerity," she remembered him saying.

And pedantic properness, she now added silently. She closed her eyes. Those years were over, and once she'd delivered Jackson's college memorabilia to Alex Stoner, she'd be free of any obligation connecting her to that period of her past. Free to get on with her new life.

"Is there something I can do for you?"

Sandy turned toward the rich baritone voice. "Yes,

I . . ." she began, then pressed the card to her lips. Whoever he was, he was gorgeous, golden, and tall. Very tall. Even at her own five feet nine inches, she had to look up at him. His feet were planted wide apart, his hands thrust deep into his pockets, and his jaw raised for any challenge that dared to confront him. She sensed immediately that he'd been watching her through those half-closed, thickly fringed eyes. The long, straight nose, squared shoulders, and broad chest pinned her in place like a royal command, but his mouth mocked that intimidating image. He had a mouth stolen from a statue. A mouth made for pagan pleasure. She blinked. Lord help her—two days away from Atlanta and she was surrendering to sensuality.

Lowering the card, she pointed it at him. "You're the man I saw at that little outdoor restaurant—"

He nodded, his steady gaze never faltering. "And you're the shopper."

Shaking her head, she laughed softly. "Oh, my. Was I that noticeable?"

His return smile was economical, and as he continued to stare, he pulled his hand from his pocket and shoved back a lock of light blond hair. She'd feel a lot more comfortable if he'd only smile the way he had in the Plaka. It would work wonders now, but he was probably busy and seeking a way out of their exchange. She winced at her next thought. Here she was, a graduate of Miss Hollingsworth's School for Young Ladies, forgetting her manners. "I'm sorry. I haven't introduced myself. I'm Sandy Patterson, and I'm afraid I'm late for my three-fifteen appointment with Alex Stoner."

"I'm Alex Stoner."

She felt her eyebrows raise, but quickly turned the involuntary gesture into a full-face smile as she stepped forward to shake his hand. He wasn't at all like the outgoing, thrill-seeking scamp Jackson had described. The diamond-in-the-rough description was blotted out by his cool and masterful presence.

"Alex, how are you?"

"Sandy Patterson? I'm afraid I don't remember ever having met you."

"You haven't, Alex. I'm Jackson Benedict's widow. I took back my maiden name." The silliest thrill coursed through her as she watched him trying to put the pieces together. Taking his hand in both of hers, she gave him a gentle squeeze. "I've really surprised you, haven't I?"

He still looked stunned, and she began to wonder if her surprise appearance had been such a great idea after all. "I know it's been two years since he died, but I did promise in my letter to give you a box of Jackson's college memorabilia." She let his hand drop from hers and pointed over her shoulder before lacing her fingers together. Only then did he respond.

"Oh, right. I do remember you writing me something about photos and a track jacket." With a perfunctory strain toward the box, he nodded.

"Those things were put away by a well-meaning friend, and I only just found them a month ago. I was cleaning out the attic and . . . You know, you don't look at all like those photos."

Close up, Sandy Patterson wasn't just pretty. She

was beautiful. Polished and gracious. Patient and warm. And that sparkle in her eyes ricocheted off every erogenous zone in his body. The truth was, she was eliciting more of his interest than any of the clever and sophisticated women he'd chosen to spend his leisure moments with. "Sorry. I've been up to my neck in paperwork. I wasn't expecting . . . you. I thought my three-fifteen appointment had to do with a business matter."

He couldn't take his eyes off her. Her soft southern accent and those sparkling root-beer eyes were a deceptively potent combination. She reminded him of girls he'd wanted and knew he couldn't have. Those good girls destined to marry men from good families. What a fool he was, believing he'd gotten rid of those old feelings. Those old desires.

Her smile was more hesitant now. "Well," she began in a whispery attempt at an apology, "I won't take up any more of your time. It was a pleasure to finally meet you. I'll just leave the box."

His carefully nurtured plan for self-preservation shriveled when he saw her turning to leave. "Please, come in. I can spare a few minutes . . . for Jackson's widow." He pushed open his office door and watched heaven move a little closer.

Knowing her scent would be a treasure he'd have to steal, he stood in the doorway, forcing her to pass close to him. He lowered his head as she entered. The soft, warm scent of honeysuckle invaded his nostrils, drifting through his brain like an illegal drug.

Avoiding her eyes, he took his place behind the desk and leaned back in the thickly upholstered executive chair. A minimum of small talk and then she'd leave, taking with her those reminders of his past. Those haunting feelings of inadequacy around the privileged.

Strangely enough, if it hadn't been for her late husband, he could still be carrying the title Stoner the Loner. Good old Jackson. Stable, reliable, and highborn, Jackson had taken a liking to Alex's streetwise, enterprising ways. The old adage that opposites attract had been the improbable basis for a friendship lasting through graduation. Did this lovely creature before him have something to do with the slow dissolution of that friendship? Let it go, he told himself. It didn't matter. Jackson was dead, and all Sandy wanted was to drop off the memorabilia and be on her way. Wasn't it?

She was fidgeting. He hated when women fidgeted. It was almost as bad as when they cried. He never knew what to do with them when that happened.

"You're traveling alone, aren't you?" His question came out sounding more like an accusation than an opener for polite conversation. He saw those root-beer eyes narrow the tiniest bit.

"Yes. How did you know?"

She was suddenly on guard and looking guilty too. Just what was she up to thousands of miles from Atlanta?

"Sandy, when I spotted you today, you were alone. And, if you don't mind me saying so, behaving incautiously."

Her pretty pink lips thinned. She laced her fingers together in her lap and tilted her chin. "Incautiously? May I ask what you mean by that?"

He adjusted the knot in his already perfectly knotted tie, then opened both hands palms up. "Forgive me, but you looked like you needed help." Not quite like the help he needed now. She didn't look in a forgiving mood. Warm and friendly Sandy Patterson had thrown in her smile for a fixed stare at his tie clasp. A long fixed stare that was probably intended to dismiss him as some inconsequential person not worthy of a response. As the uncomfortable silence continued, he fixed his own eyes on the gold chain around her neck. Part of it was hidden in her sweater, and lifting it out, she slid her fingertips over it. The totally feminine gesture stirred him, and when he realized what was happening, he could have kicked himself. Of all the women in the world, it was well-bred, proper Sandy igniting him like dry tinder. He cursed the heat flowing through him. She was exactly the kind of woman who reminded him that no matter how impressive his accomplishments were, he would never fit comfortably in a conventional family situation.

Sandy frowned. Her family and friends had been against her taking this trip, but she'd fought them on every argument. The trip was an important, if not an easy, way of announcing her choice for a new life. Damn Alex Stoner. Not only did he have her squirming under his worldly manner, he'd actually said she looked like she needed help. As if he knew exactly the next button to push, he pointed to her like a forgetful child. Perhaps he meant the move to convey informality, but it struck her as condescending.

"You do realize you were standing in the middle of

a pedestrian thoroughfare counting your money in front of everyone?"

She didn't have a chance to answer because his telephone rang, and with a quick apology he answered it. He spoke in Greek and, after a few words, placed his hand on the desk and turned partly away from her.

Just as well he'd turned away, she thought as her gaze dropped down to the desk . . . and his hand. Large and masculine, and with a hint of a tan, it contrasted beautifully with the white cuffs of his shirt. His nails were blunt cut, and his university ring, with its blue stone, nestled between the golden hair of each finger beside it. She kept on staring, mesmerized by the sensual images his hand was inspiring. A tingling sensation started between her thighs when she imagined him stroking her, arousing her to tantalizing heights of ecstasy she'd never reached before. His masterful but delicate touch had her silently gasping for air, and for more. . . . She jerked up her head when a bus backfired in the street below. If that weren't embarrassing enough, she found herself looking directly into his blue bedroom eyes. Her cheeks were stinging, her heart was pounding, and her mouth was watering. Could he have any idea what she had just been fantasizing?

He, too, looked as if he'd lost his concentration, and he hurriedly turned away from her again. Seconds later he ended his conversation and replaced the receiver. Plowing his fingers through his hair, he succeeded in rearranging it to something less than perfect and more than attractive.

"Sorry about that interruption."

Those sexy images wouldn't stop. They couldn't, not with the suddenly serious look on this demigod's face and the penetrating quality of his stare. Thank God Alex Stoner couldn't see what was on her mind. Those erotic scenes had taken over and were close to out of control. With his next words the intensity of the moment was over.

"Sandy, I hope you thought out your travel plans with some regard to personal safety. I'm surprised you're making this trip alone." He shrugged. "Of course I don't know, you could have plans to meet up with a . . . friend. I presume you must have a friend in your life by now."

As his suggestion sank in, the last of the glittering heat fell like a barometer before a storm. He'd meant a lover. Tensing, she leaned over his desk. "Where I come from, we do not presume such things. Nor would we state them if we did. We have manners, Mr. Stoner, and you are out of line." She'd moved so fast, the delicate gold chain was still shimmying against her collarbone.

"I didn't mean to insult your reputation, Sandy. But considering your naïveté, you appear to need assistance or maybe a bit of looking after."

"Looking after?" The words cut through her like a shard of glass. Those had been Jackson's favorite words when she wanted anything he didn't want. She was up on her feet. "Wrong. The last thing I need or want is looking after." Snatching her purse from the chair, she slung it over her shoulder and headed for the door. "I'll leave you to your memories. Good-bye."

She was in the hall and pushing her way out of

the front doors before he caught up with her. He pulled her back in and drew her around to face him. "Please let me apologize. I had no right to say those things."

She wasn't struggling from his grip, but she wasn't looking up at him either. He knew it wasn't necessary to keep holding her, but there was a pleasantly solid feeling to her biceps. He pictured her swimming in some country-club pool, dazzling her opponent on a nearby tennis court, or pulling him into her embrace. A hot, crazy embrace where nothing mattered but the feel of skin against skin and mouth against mouth. He closed his eyes and slowly swallowed for control. His desire to make love to Sandy Patterson was overpowering. "Look, couldn't I make it up to you for being so presumptuous?"

"Where would you find the time?" She was staring at the center of his chest. "Your secretary could barely fit me in today."

Reluctantly he removed his hands from the pink sleeves of her sweater. He raised his chin and closed his eyes. The rug-factory tour had been put off long enough, but it was getting too late to make the trip today. Then there were the preparations for his Zephyros vacation. "I have to make a day trip up north tomorrow. Maybe you could join me."

Raising her head just enough to look at him, she appeared to be thinking over his invitation. "Well, I had planned on doing a little more shopping tomorrow—"

"More shopping?" He tried teasing her with a shocked expression. "You're not finished?"

Her eyes grew wide with indignation. "No, I'm not.

I have lots of friends and relatives, and . . . why am I defending my actions to *you?* You're really getting a kick out of this, aren't you?"

He raised his eyebrows, trying to make her see the humor, but she'd have none of it. "You looked like you were having fun down there today. Like a kid in a candy shop."

"I'm not a kid in a candy shop." She reached behind her to push open the door. "I'm twenty-seven. I'm going to have a birthday this summer." Pressing her lips together and tilting her head to emphasize her seriousness, she turned and left.

He'd done it again. He'd ignited her like a pink rocket, and before he could do anything, she'd launched herself out the door and down the steps of Stoner Exports. She'd passed two pistachio vendors before he caught up with her. Walking fast beside her, he made it a point not to touch her. Who knew what she'd do on a public street?

"Sandy, I'd like to get together with you and talk."

"Sorry, I have this shopping thing to do. We tourists thrive on it. You know what I mean, Mr. Stoner. When I'm not gawking at the ancient architecture, I'm haggling over every Acropolis paperweight and string of worry beads I can find."

Staring straight ahead, she continued down the sloping sidewalk until she'd reentered the Plaka. "Are you sure you want to be seen with me? I'll have to warn you that I can pull out my camera at the least provocation." Stopping to take a breath, she repositioned her sweater sleeves, then crossed her arms over her middle. "Still want to talk?"

He ran his tongue along the inside of his cheek,

fighting back the laughter. "If you can fit me into your busy schedule."

She spent the next half minute looking at every tree and building on the block before she shook her head and began to laugh.

He laughed, too, then gave her a tentative look. "Are you always so explosive, or is this a woman thing?"

"It's a Sandy thing."

First he nodded, then changed directions and shook his head. "I don't get it."

"That's the problem, Alex. Nobody gets it."

He wanted to ask more about her last statement, but sensed this wasn't the time or place for it. He guided her to the side of the street as a three-wheel delivery van buzzed by. "You didn't come all the way to Greece just to find me. You must have other travel plans. How about Delphi? Everyone has a plan to visit Delphi."

A smile lit her face, a smile like the one she'd given him in the Plaka. "Yes, of course I plan to visit Delphi."

"Why don't you let me take you? I'm traveling that way tomorrow, and I could show you the ruins. Then we could have lunch. Talk. And, if it would interest you, I'll even throw in a tour of one of my rug factories. What do you say?"

At first she appeared skeptical, but lifting those pretty pink shoulders in an enormous shrug, she said, "Depends."

"On what?"

"How's the shopping up there?"

"Great. The area's well known for its pottery

and . . ." Her wide-eyed expression was serious. Too serious. She was teasing him without mercy. He leaned his shoulder against a stone wall and laughed silently. What a warmly satisfying feeling *that* was.

Two

Stopping on their way up the footpath, Sandy removed her backpack, dropped it to the ground, and pivoted for a better look at Delphi. The sun blazed above them, showering the ruins with crystal-pure light. Books and pictures hadn't done it justice, she mused, as she experienced the mystical power of the ancient site. She pulled in another lungful of cool mountain air. Mystical power, or was it the effect of slightly less oxygen?

Laughing softly, she turned to Alex. "I've never felt so far from Atlanta in all my life."

His smile was one of amusement, and the silent laughter brightening his eyes embarrassed her. He probably thought she looked like a giddy child on her first trip to the circus, or that kid in a candy shop again. Confusion whirled inside her. That's exactly how she did feel, exhilarated with the moment and wanting to share it with someone . . . special. For a fraction of a second their stares connected, but just as quickly she looked away.

This magnetic pull she felt toward him was incredible. It was getting stronger every time she looked at him, every time he looked at her. She winced inwardly. Could he sense what it was doing to her physically? she wondered, and if he could, was that the reason for his laughing eyes?

Looking back at the ruins, she attempted to untangle the ribbons of nerves knotting in her stomach. A potent case of infatuation, that's all this was. Well, she wasn't so green that she couldn't understand its causes. The excitement of traveling alone in a foreign country couldn't always keep her safe from an occasional moment of loneliness. And Alex, with his golden-god looks, was right beside her. There was also the language. Except for a few food names, she didn't understand a word of Greek, and his mastery of the rhythmic syllables fascinated her. What little he'd told her of himself was fascinating too. He was a self-made man. With no one to back him and no close family to hand him a business, he'd built his export company single-handedly.

He'd propped a foot on a stone block and was resting his corded and well-muscled forearms on his thigh. That hand she'd studied so well yesterday hadn't lost its ability to stir her. His mouth too. His beautiful mouth. And his tongue . . . as he skimmed it expertly over her breasts and belly. She closed her eyes. *Sex,* she thought boldly, *or the lack of it.* Her close girlfriends had all agreed. "Sooner or later, Sandy, the need will come back." If they only knew. She shifted her weight from one foot to another as she tried to force her thoughts away from those disturbing images. Her path into a world of independence, not to mention her morals, had no place for one-night stands or vacation flings. Yet something beneath Alex's handsome exterior, something beyond the normal mating needs of man and woman, something poignant and compelling, was tugging her to him.

"Sandy?"

She felt her heart skipping beats again. "Yes?"

"You're not the only one feeling it."

Short of fleeing down the footpath and hijacking a tour bus back to Athens, there was no escape.

"Really?" Her voice was a whisper on the breeze.

"Delphi packs a pretty powerful wallop, no matter how many times I've been here."

She forced a weak smile. At least he wasn't adding fuel to her fiery infatuation by whispering something romantic. "A wallop. Definitely a wallop."

"Yes. I'd almost forgotten how it hits a person the first time. Your face, your eyes, they bring it back to me."

She repeated the words silently. *Your face, your eyes, they bring it back to me.* The sweet simplicity of his words settled softly into her heart. Squinting at the ruins below, she pulled out her newly purchased map of Delphi and began unfolding it.

"Alex, what is that circle of marble blocks? Do you know?" Before she could turn to look at him, he was beside her, his breath warm against her cheek. That would have been hard enough to handle, but when he touched her hand to steady the map, a stinging rush of blood flooded every sensitive spot on her body. He smelled like leather and limes and, best of all, his own natural scent. Clean and masculine.

If she lifted her mouth, and he lowered his—Lord, would this day ever end?

At that moment a puff of wind snatched the map from one of her hands. Her reaction was immediate, and so were the consequences.

Digging her heels into the path, she bent her knees and grabbed at the air. His arms went around her waist in the same instant she started her slow skid. Her inelegant maneuvers were no match for his strength. Still, she fought for purchase, praying she would right herself before she had to lean back into his embrace. Stones scattered everywhere, and the soft brown dirt began filling her shoes. She knew she was going to lose with either choice when he stepped closer and she felt her backside burrowing against his masculinity. Why did it have to feel so damn *good?*

"Relax, I've got you."

"I'm okay," she lied.

He wasn't letting go.

Defeat never felt so fine as she closed her eyes, let go of the flapping map, and leaned back. His navy cotton sweater did little to soften the hard planes of his body. She consoled herself with the notion that the worst of it was over. It wasn't. The soles of her shoes slipped over several more stones, and her feet went out from under her. As she settled closer to the ground, first his arm, then his hand, slid over one breast. She felt his fingertips kneading the soft mound, then flattening it to her chest. The contact lasted less than two seconds, but it was enough to send an electrifying current throughout her entire body.

"I told you to relax," he said, an air of apology apparent in his voice.

She brushed nonexistent dust from her sleeves. "And I told you I was okay."

"But you weren't."

She opened her mouth to argue, but to do so would make her look foolish. And that she already looked. Or maybe only funny. "Well, thanks for saving my life."

The words were melodramatic in nature and—she realized too late—a perfect lead-in for his comeback.

"It was my pleasure."

She'd set herself up for that one. Staring at the dusty hill, she dragged her backpack off the steep incline and into the grassy ruins. "Well, anyway, that was a good map."

"I can see it from here. Will you be okay if I go after it?"

Slitting her eyes, she tightened her jaw, making her words barely understandable. "I'll brace myself against this cornerstone and try to hold on until you get back."

He started down the hill, then stopped his jaunty descent to look up at her. "Sandy?"

She looked up from emptying her shoe. "Yes?"

"Don't hesitate to call me if you feel yourself slipping again."

Sinking down on the grass, she couldn't help grinning over the wink accompanying his words. Despite the recent embarrassment when his hand touched her breast, she was glad to see him relaxing with her. Although he'd been trying hard to hide it, she was beginning to recognize hints of a great sense of humor. And it was about time. He'd been a perfect gentleman on the drive up from Athens. Stiflingly perfect. During the drive he'd listened attentively as she told him about Jackson's civic, social, and political accomplishments. About their house and his low golf score. Even that he'd been part owner of a racehorse. But when she should have been telling him about Jackson's final days, a gaping silence filled the space between them. Unless Alex asked outright about that time, she had no desire to bring up those painful memories. He'd finally taken the initiative and told her how his own vacation to Greece had become the major transition period of his life. In search of the perfect flokati rug, he ended up, two years later, exporting them all over the world.

While she waited for him to return with the map, she pulled out her sketch pad and was well into her composition by the time he'd returned. As he tucked the map into her backpack, she looked up from her sketching. "Thanks. I'll be through with this in just a second. It's probably time to leave for your rug factory."

He sat down, stretching out those long chino-clad legs of his alongside hers and planting his elbow in a clump of grass. "Don't hurry. There's plenty of time." His cheek rested in the cup of his hand as he watched the pencil sketch taking shape.

"A hobby?"

"Oh, I couldn't have this as a hobby."

"Couldn't? Hmmm."

His questioning tone begged to hear more, but when she didn't offer, he pulled off his sweater, bunched it behind him, and, reclining, closed his eyes. It would have been a luxury to be able to accept his companionable silence, because she'd had little of that in her life. She lifted her pencil from the pad. If she didn't give him an explanation now, he might ask a more direct question she wouldn't be able to sidestep.

"I guess I meant to say I've always wanted this to be more than a hobby. For years the only drawings I did were posters for the garden club. You see, I was kept—I mean, was quite busy as Jackson's wife."

She waited for his reaction, but when there was none, she dismissed the fear. So much was behind her, and there was no reason to look back. With a little more wistfulness than she would have liked, she said, "I'd forgotten how good it feels to put a pencil to paper and draw what I want to draw."

His words came muffled in drowsiness. "Well, this is the place to make pretty pictures." He drew in a long breath, then exhaled contentedly. "Where are you planning to travel, by the way?"

"The islands."

From the corner of her eye she saw him raise up on both elbows.

"Which islands?"

"Mykonos. Santorini. Crete." Twisting her head to face him, she noticed the tiniest signs of alertness that hadn't been there a moment ago. She also noticed pieces of grass stuck in his collar and a lock of hair dangling on the side of his forehead. She picked a stem from his collar, then looked into his sexy, bottomless eyes. "And maybe I'll come back here. This place does pack a wallop," she said, surprising herself with the whispery quality of her own voice.

He was the first to look away as he turned toward her sketch pad. Pulling himself into a sitting position beside her, he took the pad and studied it. "You kept the power in the toppled columns, but softened them with shadows. They look like sleeping giants." He looked at her with a different kind of awareness when he passed the pad back to her lap. "Sandy, you're much too good to call this a hobby."

Then it happened again. His fingers brushed hers, sending sparks up her arm and through her body. No, she told herself, it was his compliment and not his touch that warmed her. Anyone would be thrilled by such sincerity. Even if it came from the devil himself. "Thank you."

Putting away the sketch pad, she clasped her hands around her knees and looked away from him. A yellow butterfly circled a clump of bright red poppies, then suddenly took off. Not that she wanted to boast, but it might keep her mind off him if she told him she'd been accepted by one of the most prestigious art schools in Chicago. She turned to tell him when a group of raucous children rushed by, sending sprays of pebbles and dust everywhere. Although she didn't understand Greek, their message was instantly understandable. They were out of the classroom on a glorious spring day, and their attitude was infectious. Waving away the dust, she coughed theatrically. "I believe Delphi's being invaded by the barbarians again."

Alex looked up the path toward the shouting children. "Nah. Too short for barbarians."

She giggled at his quick comeback. Some of the children were singing the explicit words of a Madonna song. Alex smiled and shook his head. The words became more explicit. Soon Sandy was laughing, and he joined her. His masculine timbre covered her like a warm, familiar hug until the last of it, along with the song, echoed down the ruins.

He was twisting his university ring around and around his finger as they continued a playful game of staring each other down. They were completely alone now, and she leaned toward him on her forearm. "I'll bet you were a very naughty schoolboy."

Never breaking their gaze, he nodded in serious agreement. "Very naughty."

Mesmerized by his low voice and the sparkling blue of his eyes, she whispered back, "How naughty?"

"This naughty."

Cupping her chin in his fingers, he brushed his lips against hers, then pulled back. His kiss was the last thing she'd expected, but her own response surprised her more. "That's not so naughty."

Without a word he slipped his arm around her and drew her close for another try. He began the kiss, like the first, with a passing brush at her lips. *It's only a kiss,* she told herself, about the time he began gently nipping at her mouth. The sensation of his touch spilled through her like liquid sunshine, and soon her mouth tingled for the attention he was lavishing at its corners. *I can stop this anytime I feel like it.* She closed her eyes. With a slight suction he sealed her ips to his. Dipping his tongue into her mouth, he probed with a swirling swiftness that brought her breasts to pebbly peaks. He'd been polite. He'd been helpful. He'd even been funny, but this was a different Alex Stoner. Passionate. Inviting. Arousing. And aroused. He pressed his length against her as he continued the kiss. Penetrating deeply with his tongue, he rhythmically stroked the sensitive recesses of her mouth. She groaned with the overwhelming pleasure he was giving her. No one had ever kissed her like this. She'd never imagined a kiss could be like this.

Alex Stoner was about to go over the brink, and if it hadn't been for that sound she was making, he'd have forgotten where he was and whom he was with. Breaking the kiss, he lifted his head and stared into her half-closed eyes. Their longing made his heart cringe and his arousal stronger. She smelled like honeysuckle on a hot summer day and tasted like it too. Honeysuckle. That fragile-looking vine that flourished on white picket fences and up trellised terraces on the right side of the tracks. Why the hell was she with him?

He released her, then sat up and reached into his shirt pocket for a cigarette. "Naughty enough for you?"

With flaming cheeks, she sat up and pushed her fingers through her hair. "Quite."

He knew he'd wounded her with his sarcasm, but it would be wrong to allow her to read anything into the moment. Having gotten way out of hand, the kiss had become intense, passionate, and much too revealing. Angry with himself, he bit off the question, "Why the hell did you come to Greece?"

She didn't bother to face him. "I told you. I'd always wanted to see Greece, and I'd promised to give you those things of Jackson's."

Taking her by the shoulders, he twisted her around to face him. "The real reason."

Determination glowed in her eyes. "The real reason, Alex, as trite as it might sound, is that I'm here to test myself. To see what I'm capable of. To find some answers. No matter how well intentioned some people are, they haven't any right to tell me what I can't do or to force me to live any way other than my own way. And maybe I don't know what my own way is yet, but it's time I found out."

Confusion and embarrassment clouded her eyes, and earnestness took over where anger left off. Her soft southern drawl wrenched at his gut.

"Alex, I have so many questions."

He looked her over. "What questions? Sandy, you have everything back there in Atlanta. You're a respectable member of your community. You have friends, and a family who care about you. A place you call home. It sounds pretty damned perfect to me. So rather than traipsing around the Greek islands, kissing naughty boys, I think you'd be much better off, much safer, if you were back in Atlanta in that perfect life."

Her laugh was short and sharp. "I thought for a moment there that you might be someone who would understand."

"Understand what?"

"I had a perfect life—now I want a real one."

Shrugging free from his hold, she stood up. "And who asked you, anyway?" Grabbing her backpack, she stepped over his legs, out onto the path, and promptly slipped and fell. The pain in her wrist was immediate and astounding.

"Alex, it's a little scratch."

He helped her from the car and over to the low stone wall bordering the outdoor restaurant. "Sit."

She cradled her left wrist in her right hand, moving it only when he placed the first-aid kit in her lap. "It stopped bleeding ten minutes ago. See?" She held up her wrist. Several people in the restaurant waiting line craned to look, but Alex didn't. "I know your wrist has stopped bleeding." He knelt on the flagstones in front of her. "But your leg's just getting started."

"My *leg?* I didn't know—" Before she could stop him, he'd ripped her slacks from ankle to knee. "Good gracious! What are you doing? Alex, everyone is looking."

He picked her up from the overlook wall and carried her to the far corner. "Unless you want to struggle in the ladies' room with your one good hand, or drop your slacks behind those bushes, this is the only way to get a good look at the damage." Lifting the torn cloth, he let out a low whistle. "I see you've got Skinned Knee One-oh-one down pat."

Holding her wrist away from her lap, Sandy leaned over to have a look. She was nose to nose with him. "It doesn't hurt . . . much. Really."

"It will when I start picking out the gravel." By the way her eyes widened, he knew she was lying about how much it hurt. She was in pain, and he had the overwhelming need to stop it. True, the knee injury wasn't serious, but he'd done something quite similar to himself, and it had stung like hell. He closed his hand over her good knee.

"Wait here. I'll get something to clean this with."

While he was gone, she carefully inspected the knee again. A little antiseptic and a four-by-four bandage would take care of it. The injured wrist was something else. Her gaze dropped to her throbbing joint. She hated to think what damage she'd done to it. With a loud sign she turned to the view behind her. The Gulf of Corinth was a beautiful soothing blue, but she wished she could look at it without wincing. Her trip had only just begun and difficulties were piling up at an alarming rate. A messy knee, a possibly sprained wrist, and . . Alex. Even the calmest, quietest moments spent with him seemed to resonate with tension. He'd touched just about every emotion she was capable of, and a few she hadn't known about. And that kiss. She'd held back from active participation, but he'd taken that as a challenge. Then, just as she'd begun to get into the action, he'd pulled away and resumed treating her like a child. The man was simply infuriating.

Alex plunked a plastic liter bottle of water on the stone surface next to her. "Sandy?"

With lips pressed firmly together, she tore her gaze from the gulf. If he wanted another argument, she'd be pleased to participate.

"Sandy, I'm sorry this happened. I should have warned you—"

The words weren't what set her off. His tone was calming and patronizing, and if he didn't stop treating her like a four-year-old, she'd scream.

"Let me assure you, this is the result of my own carelessness, not yours, Alex."

While she was speaking, he'd removed her shoe and sock. "Carelessness," he repeated.

"That's right. My carelessness."

He picked up the water bottle and twisted the top until it opened with a crack. "Your honesty is refreshing. It's also enlightening, if you'd only listen to yourself." Lifting her injured wrist, he poured water over it.

"What do you mean?"

Slipping his hand beneath her injured knee, he bypassed her question with a firm command. "Hold still. This one's going to hurt."

He poured half a bottle of water over her knee. "Those stones are washing right out." Making a satisfied clicking sound from one side of his mouth, he smiled up at her. She didn't see it. Her eyes were closed, her posture rigid, and she was sucking in air through clenched teeth.

His tone changed. "Sandy, I'm sorry I'm hurting you. That's all I seem capable of doing to you."

Opening her eyes, she took the bottle from him and placed it beside her. "You didn't do anything to me. I told you, it was my own carelessness."

He took a spray can of antiseptic and a package of bandages from the first-aid kit. "And that only proves you can't travel alone."

"But I *am* traveling alone."

"Not any longer." He gave the can of antiseptic a quick shake, then liberally sprayed her knee. Reaching for her wrist, he gently positioned it away from her lap and sprayed that too. "There's no way you can continue your vacation now."

She'd just about gotten the courage to test the edges of her injury with one fingertip when she jerked up her head. "Alex, I'm not going back. Not yet, anyway."

Blowing on her knee, he quickly taped a bandage over the cut. "How do you think you're going to manage? That's a superficial cut on your knee, but look at the wrist. How many suitcases do you have?"

"Three."

"Three? Plus your backpack and purse? And who'll be carrying all this?"

"Well, I'll, I'll . . . I'll tip the cabdrivers well. And the bellboys."

He shook his head. "You're planning on heading out to the islands. Cabdrivers won't take your bags up the gangplank and onto the ferry, and once you're on the islands, you'll have to get yourself to your hotel."

"Alex, I can manage this," she insisted. Her jolly tone didn't appear to move him. She looked around, then spotted the half liter of water. "See?" Grasping the bottle with her injured wrist, she managed to lift it several inches before dropping it with a startled cry.

The plastic bottle hit the stones just as pain gathered in her stomach like a frozen bowling ball. Her forehead and upper lip broke into a sweat as she doubled over. Alex was beside her in a flash, holding her head against his chest while she gasped for breath. When her breathing slowed, he lifted the wrist for closer inspection, then looked up with an accusing expression.

"Just what did you think you were doing?"

"I didn't know—Ouch! Stop touching it."

Alex stuffed the second bandage into the first-aid kit, clicked it shut, and stood up. "Let's go."

"I'm not very hungry. Why don't you get in line?"

"Forget lunch. We have to go."

She nodded slowly, surprised at his sudden change in attitude. Then she remembered where he had to be today. "The rug factory. Right, I didn't want you to be late for your inspection."

"The rug factory is last on my list, if it's there at all now." He stuffed her sock in his pocket and slipped her shoe on her foot.

"Wait a minute. Wait just a minute." If he thought he was getting her on a plane to Atlanta . . . "Forget it, Alex. I don't care how many times you whack yourself in the forehead, you're not taking me to the airport. I meant it when I said I'm not going back to Atlanta just yet. You can't make me go."

"Much as I think you should go, I know I can't make you. Sandy, I'm taking you to a doctor."

"A doctor?" Her wrist was positively throbbing with pain now. She gave in with a weak smile. "I suppose it wouldn't hurt."

An hour later she watched as Alex listened attentively to the doctor at the local clinic. The conversation was almost inaudible from across the room, but since she didn't understand Greek, it didn't matter.

Alex had already translated the diagnosis. Sprained wrist. As the minutes ticked by, her heart sank lower. And lower still. As much as she hated admitting it, Alex was right. There was no way she could continue her trip alone. Whether it was because of the pain or the decision she'd been forced to make, she felt tears welling up in her eyes. This wasn't going to be the end of her life, but then it wasn't going to be the new beginning she'd planned either. She smacked one fat tear from her jaw. Damn, why did it have to be now?

Alex was scratching his head and nodding. How many instructions, she wondered, came with a sprained wrist? The naughty schoolboy had vanished, and in his place was a concerned and determined man. A gentle and tender man who cared enough to look away when he saw that tear slide down her face.

The doctor walked over to her and patted her shoulder. After saying something in Greek, he smiled, then left them alone in the stark white room.

Alex looked as if he'd resigned himself to slow torture as he turned to face her. "That settles it, Sandy. The doctor and I agree. Your plans have definitely been changed."

She tried smiling, but the brave attempt was a lousy charade. At least her tears had disappeared. "I think I knew that before we got here."

Alex smiled then for the first time. She had set aside her feistiness, for the time being at least, and was facing up to what she conceded to be the inevitable.

"Maybe we could stop at the travel agent across the street and change my ticket." She swallowed back more tears. "That way we could pick up my things at the hotel in Athens, and you could drop me at the airport. There are plenty of flights—"

"Hold on there. I said your plans have been changed, but I didn't say to what."

"What are you talking about?"

"According to the doctor, if you keep the splint on and don't lift any more bottled water, in about two or three weeks you should have full use of it. The choice is yours. You can go back to Atlanta and sit around Peachtree Street like Miss Melanie, or you can do what Scarlett would have done."

She smiled in spite of her confusion. "What's that?"

"You can come with me to my place on Zephyros. I've already planned to stay a few weeks anyway. It will give you plenty of time to recuperate."

"I couldn't. I absolutely could not impose on you a minute more."

He couldn't believe he was attempting to convince a woman to come to Zephyros. "I'm not going to kidnap you, but think about this before you answer. It's your choice. Back to Atlanta and all that perfection, or on to Zephyros," he said, before leaning on the examination table, "with the real Alex Stoner. What'll it be?"

She nibbled the inside of her lip as she looked at the plastic splint encasing her wrist. She could handle one day with Alex. But three weeks with this man who stimulated her on every level imaginable? His nearness was as much of a challenge as his words were. "Are you sure I won't be imposing?"

"Only if you can't make up your mind."

Three weeks? Three unpredictable weeks when anything could happen? Wasn't that what she'd come for? Wasn't that what her new life was supposed to be about? She smiled. "Then, the real Alex Stoner, if you please."

He nodded once and carefully helped her down from the table.

"Alex?"

"Changed your mind?"

"No. I just wondered what the doctor said to me before he left the room."

"He said, 'Welcome to Greece.'"

Three

By the time Bertram MacDougall walked into the Zephyros airport terminal, Alex's patience was already worn thin. He'd had time to reconsider his impulsive invitation to Sandy. While he knew he could handle the next few weeks, he wasn't so certain she would be able to do the same. Alex's tightly knit group of expatriate friends weren't exactly the country-club set. Their unpredictability was enough to send most "settled" people over the wall.

He looked down at Sandy, curled and sleeping in a molded chair, then up at his friend crossing the small terminal. Bertram was wearing his kilt. Alex closed his eyes. "Where's Niko?"

"And hello to you, too, Alexander. Your gracious housekeeper called before supper to tell me her husband's truck hit a goat and would I please fetch Mr. Alex at the airport. I'm verra sorry for the delay."

"You'd better plan on dying a day early."

The six-foot-four-inch Scotsman shared his toothy grin and a wave with the remaining terminal personnel before he hooked his thumbs in the top of his kilt and closed one eye at Alex. "And why is that?"

"Because you'll be late to your own funeral if you don't." Alex tapped his watch face. "You're through with your supper by eight. It's now nine. What have you been up to for the last half hour?"

Bertram slapped him on the shoulder, then gave his hand a vehement shake. "Well, if you must know, I've been fine-tunin' me fiddle." He pulled back for a better look at Sandy.

Alex shoved a lock of hair off his forehead. *Here we go*, he thought.

"And, by the looks of her," his friend continued, "you've been fine-tunin' yours too, laddie." Screwing his mouth into mock disapproval, Bertram picked up several suitcases and headed for the door. "It's a shame you had to break her wrist when you were doin' it. There's such a thing as technique."

Alex closed his eyes. From the moment he'd decided to bring Sandy, he knew he'd be in for a ribbing. Scooping her up, he followed his friend to the minivan, illegally parked by the front door, and settled into the front seat with her. When Bertram had stored the baggage, he climbed in by Alex and started the engine.

"It's about time you shared your fine house with someone."

"Bertram, you know damn well how I feel about this. I work hard at my business, so when I schedule time out here, I don't want to have to entertain someone every minute. Besides, the last time I brought someone out here, she didn't want to leave."

"Laddie, it's those signals you're always sending to the lassies that's put you in this fix."

"I'm not in a fix. What signals?"

"You're a bachelor who's determined he'd like to stay that way. You're also rich, good-looking, and you don't go without a lover for long. Think about the challenge you're presenting to those lassies."

Alex stared out the windshield. The gist of what Bertram had said was true. Right from the beginning he always made it clear to his lovers that he wasn't interested in a long-term commitment. More times than not, they'd taken his words as a challenge. There was that one time he felt certain the woman understood, so he'd brought her to Zephyros. Before the month was up, she'd shipped her entire wardrobe, her art collection, and her Afghan out to the island.

"I'm not challenging this one, Bertram. Her name's Sandy Patterson. She's the widow of an old friend. She had an accident up at Delphi, and I offered her my guest room until she's strong enough to continue her trip."

Bertram shifted gears, then looked out his open window as he pulled away. "Sandy Patterson. And if Sandy Patterson's husband were to rise from his grave, would you be cuddlin' him so close?"

Alex shot a warning glance. "Bertram."

"Well, you could have stretched her out in the back, lad. It's a wonder you haven't cut off the circulation in your—"

"Bertram!"

The Scotsman roared with laughter, causing Sandy to moan, then nuzzle under Alex's chin.

He kept a warning eye on Bertram as he patted Sandy's thigh. No man could ask for a better friend, but Bertram had the bawdiest sense of humor of anyone Alex knew. Alex closed his eyes and rested his chin against Sandy's forehead. "She's on pain medication—which is what you'll be on if you don't stuff it."

"Hurtin', is she?" As they approached the one hairpin turn on the hill road, Bertram slowed the van. He usually took the turn on two wheels.

Grateful for the letup in his ribbing, Alex asked about the second closest thing to Bertram's heart. "How's the gallery? Sales picking up yet, or are you still waiting for the summer cruise ships?"

With almost as much gusto as he'd given to ribbing Alex, Bertram spent the rest of the drive filling Alex in on his art gallery. Half listening, Alex slipped his hand under Sandy's wrist, holding it in what he believed was a more comfortable position. She'd fought against taking pain medication all through the afternoon and early evening. When Alex told her the short flight to Zephyros would be a bumpy one, she finally gave in and took the pills.

Like a curled-up kitten intent on slumber, she slept through the noisy greeting by Alex's housekeeper. As Eleni took charge of a sleeping Sandy, now deposited on the guest-room bed, Bertram and Alex unloaded the van.

"The clan expects you at seven tomorrow night. Don't forget to bring your girl."

"She's not my girl."

"Aye." Bertram shut the back of the van, then climbed into the driver's seat. "Bring your widow friend, then. Taro knows you're back, and he's making something with a black butter sauce."

"Bertram?"

"Speak."

He shook his head. "Nothing. Just wanted to thank you for picking us up tonight."

"Now, laddie, don't go all soft on me," he said with a fake scowl. "Besides, I owed you, didn't I? That last bit of gallery business you sent my way kept me going through the winter."

Alex remained in the driveway long after the minivan's tail lights disappeared. The sound of breaking waves and the scent of the sea filled the air around him, and a sense of peace descended over him. So Taro was making his black butter sauce for tomorrow night's get-together. Bertram was wearing his kilt, which meant he'd been romancing a new lady in his life. And his housekeeper's husband had hit a goat. It sounded like life on Zephyros was rolling along at its usual pace. The interesting part of the reunion would be Sandy's reaction to "the clan," Bertram's favorite description of them. Chuckling to himself, he turned to go in.

"Mr. Alex?"

"Yes, Eleni, how's our guest?"

His short, rotund housekeeper smiled knowingly. "Pretty. Very pretty. It's pleasant for you, no? To bring a very pretty lady to Zephyros."

Better, he decided, to move past her innuendo and into his bedroom for a good night's sleep. "Pleasant," he agreed. "Is she sleeping?"

"Soon. She took the pills you gave me. Mr. Alex, she has pretty nightclothes." Eleni's calm expression was meant to tease him. "Come, I will show you."

He patted her gently on the shoulder. "No, thank you. That will be all for tonight."

"Niko is coming to walk me. You don't have to drive me. Mr. Alex, her accident will be healthy soon?"

The concern in her eyes touched him. "Yes, her accident will be healthy soon. Two or three weeks, the doctor says."

"You are a kind man to bring her here. She will thank you. Welcome home, Mr. Alex," she said, before closing the front door behind her.

Alex went to the guest room, telling himself it was only right to check on Sandy. With only a faint light from the bathroom, it was difficult to see her at first, but he had no trouble hearing her restless movements. The tender emotions welling up inside him were unsettling. He forced himself to interpret them as a call to action. Sandy didn't need her recuperation period extended by further injury, so he found another pillow and placed it under her wrist. Before his eyes could adjust to the dim light, he retreated from her bedside. The last thing he needed was a better look at her breasts under that gauzy nightgown.

Sandy checked that all her buttons were buttoned, then reached for the door handle. She managed to close her fingers all the way around the brass lever before withdrawing them. She stared down at the floor, then took an extraordinary amount of time straightening the corner of the throw rug with her toe. Her hesitant manner was beginning to irritate her.

"For goodness' sake," she chided herself. This wasn't the end of the world. If she couldn't remember undressing for bed last night, then there could be only one explanation. Alex had been the one to remove her clothes, dress her in her diaphanous negligee, and tuck her into bed. Circumstances had necessitated those actions, and if she mentioned them at all to Alex, or if he did to her, she would thank him for his efforts. After all, it couldn't be much fun undressing dead weight. Could it?

Saying a silent prayer that her cheeks weren't flaming, she flipped a lock of hair behind her ear and opened the door. It took her a few minutes to find the kitchen, but the search turned out to be pleasant and revealing. The rambling house was inviting in its fashionably rustic simplicity. Large and small flokatis and woven rugs were scattered around the marble and wood floors of the sun-filled rooms. Unlike the fragile antiques she'd lived with, Alex's furniture looked comfortable and indestructible. The only thing in common with her home in Atlanta was the choice of fine-quality appointments.

"Alex?" Her voice echoed off the thickly plastered walls, timbered supports and ceilings, and colorful Grecian tiles. When he didn't answer, she gave up her house search and stepped out onto the patio. The remains of his breakfast were still on the table there, along with a place setting, presumably for her. As she drank a glass of orange juice, she looked around the patio, hoping to keep her mind off last night. This part of the house jutted close to the cliff and the towering rock formations rising straight up from the shore. At the far end of the spacious patio was a bright blue railing, with an entrance to a set of steps leading down to the sea. Picking up a piece of toast, she went to the top of the steps and started down.

Halfway down and past a dogleg turn, she saw the thick crescent of sand hugging the sparkling Aegean. The sun was already high in a cloudless blue sky, its reflections a scattering of broken gold glass on the aquamarine water. She wanted to set up her easel and capture the breathtaking scene:

Towering rocks and cloudless sky, the soft beige beach and jewel toned-water . . . and Alex as he broke through the surface. . . .

The artist inside her appreciated the unique quality of the light bouncing around the little cove, but the woman inside centered her appreciation on the way it played on Alex. Sinking slowly to the steps, she welcomed in the details. He was standing waist-deep in the water and facing away from her. Sandy propped her good arm on her knee and leaned her chin into the cup of her hand. The definition of his muscles and the straight indentation of his spine were enough to inspire any artist, but something else set him apart. Rivulets of water cascaded from his hair and down over his shoulders and arms and back. Water and sun worked together, glazing him in a glorious gold light. When he reached up to rest his hands on his head, the muscle definition in his back and shoulders begged to be reproduced by her paintbrushes. Suddenly he leaned sideways and into the water, disappearing for a long time, then breaking through the sun-dappled surface again.

His boyish antics had brought him closer to shore this time.

It would be just a matter of seconds before he saw her . . . spying on him. Jumping to her feet, she waved and shouted his name. "Good morning!"

Soon he was waving too. "How's the wrist?" he shouted.

Holding up her hand for him to wait until she joined him, she climbed down the rest of the steps and crossed the sand to the water's edge.

"My wrist is fine."

"Did that pillow help? I thought you'd be less likely to roll over if I propped up your wrist."

So he had undressed her. An uncomfortable silence hung between them. She licked nervously at her lips, then decided to get it over with. "Yes, that pillow did the trick. Thank you for, uh, getting me to bed last night."

He rubbed water from his mouth, then shrugged. "Don't you remember? My housekeeper did that. I just propped your wrist."

"Your housekeeper? Oh, yes, of course I remember."

He was giving her a doubtful look that was slowly turning into a knowing smile. She had to change the subject. Now.

"How's the water this morning?"

"Would you believe, it's cold at first, but once you're in—"

"—it warms right up," she said along with him.

Her gaze drifted lower. The gentle waves lapping at his stomach soon had a hypnotic effect on her. Starting at his breastbone, thin arrowheads of wet hair ran down his stomach and disappeared into a dark blond whorl around his navel. After each breaking lap, she noticed, the arrowheads continued lower.

"Sandy?"

She looked up to catch a curious grin growing on his face.

"Yes?"

He urged her toward him. "Come on in." He made it sound like a reasonable suggestion. Something close to "Have a seat."

Opening her arms, she looked down at her clothes, then back to him.

He *tsk*ed in disapproval. "Where's your sense of adventure?"

"But I'm not wearing my suit."

"No problem. Neither am I."

She fixed her eyes on the horizon over his right shoulder. "I—I knew that." Flustered, she quickly lowered her gaze to her splint. "It's my wrist."

He pushed forward in the water. "Well, if you came all the way down here, I guess I'll have to have a look. I thought you said it was fine."

She took a step sideways. "The splint's come loose. I mean, I don't want to get it wet. You don't have to come out now." Her words ran together like stampeding horses, but Alex reached the finish line first. Churning up a screen of white water with both his hands, he was out of the water and standing beside her before she could catch her breath. He'd splashed her from head to toe, and when she stopped blinking, she stared at him in disbelief. Hanging dangerously low on his hips was a pair of green-and-blue swim trunks. "You tricked me!"

He slipped his thumbs inside the waistband and began lowering the wet trunks. "Never let it be said Alex Stoner tricked a lady."

"Don't you dare."

He took them down another half inch.

She backed up. "Stop that!"

He did, but only to peruse her with a mischievous gleam in his eyes. "You knew I wasn't wearing a suit, did you?" he asked, waving a scolding finger at her.

Relieved that he'd pulled the waistband back to its proper place, she let down her guard. "At first I thought you had, but . . . well . . . that's beside the point! You led me to believe you weren't."

"Are you always so trusting?"

She picked at the Velcro fasteners on her splint. Back in Atlanta no one would dare bother her—Jackson's widow, Patterson's daughter, the garden-club artist—with such picayune antics.

"Not going to tell me?" Picking up his towel from a nearby rock, he began rubbing his chest. "Truth is, I usually don't wear anything in the water. I wore these because I wasn't sure how you'd take my libertine lifestyle if you happened to find your way down here this morning." He finished drying, then knotted the towel around his waist and moved closer. Taking the splinted wrist in his hands, he began a readjustment of the fasteners. "How's that? Too tight? Wave your fingers."

She waved her fingers. "No. It feels better now. Thank you."

"Sandy?"

He was still holding her splint, his fingertips cool and soothing against her sun-warmed hand. She raised her eyes without raising her head. His lashes were spiked with water, he needed a shave, and his eyes were still brimming with boyish mischief. He took her breath away.

"Wondering what it's like without your suit?"

"No." But she was.

"Yes, you are. Everyone wonders at one time or another."

Her eyes were locked with his as he continued.

"This is my beach. My private beach. No one gets onto this beach unless it's through my property up there. Do you understand why I'm telling you this?"

She shook her head.

"If you stay here long enough, your inhibitions will drop out of sight, like stones tossed in the sea."

"I don't think so," she whispered.

"It's true, Sandy. Most people on this island swim nude. Sooner or later you'll look at them and start to think about it. About how it feels. All that water flowing over you, being one with the sea. It's exhilarating. Almost spiritual." He leaned closer, his voice low and inviting. Frighteningly inviting. "It's some kind of wonderful."

He wasn't teasing anymore. He meant every word of it. "Alex, I've never taken my clothes off in public, and I don't intend to start now."

"This isn't public. It's private."

He kept on smiling. Waiting. Challenging her to cross a line she'd been taught never to cross. She looked up at the surrounding walls of rocks, then at the aquamarine water turning to a frothy line at her feet. And Alex's. There were certain things good girls just didn't do. Withdrawing her hand, she stepped away from him. "Never. Not in your lifetime or mine."

After lunch he showed her his small library. When he explained he had to get to some paperwork he'd brought from Athens, she thanked him for showing her the book-lined room. She didn't bother to tell him that the last thing she'd come to Greece to do was to read old issues of *National Geographic*, wool-production reports from New Zealand, or even his collection of best-selling hardcovers. She had come with plans to paint, and the light on the partially shaded patio was too inviting to ignore. After managing to assemble her easel with her one working wrist and carefully setting out her supplies, she began to paint the seascape visible from the far end of the patio. She felt an excitement building as various blues and creamy beiges were delicately blended into an impressionistic view of the Aegean. She'd been right to think Greece would inspire her to do better work, but she'd never imagined that it could happen so fast. When she stood to arch her back and stretch two hours later, she saw Alex leaning against the doorway.

"How long have you been here?"

"About ten minutes. You certainly have a gift for concentration." He pushed off the doorjamb and came toward her. "Let's have a look."

To allow a look at a hasty sketch was one thing, but once she'd put paint on the canvas, no one was allowed a peek. Shielding the easel with her body, she pleaded, "Please don't ask to see it."

He gave her a pitiful smile. "Pretty bad, huh? And you were doing so well with that sketch at Delphi. Don't worry. Tonight we're going to a party with some friends of mine. I'll introduce you to Bertram. He owns a gallery on the waterfront, and maybe you could find something there to take back with you. What's so funny?"

"Nothing at all." She took him by the elbow and walked him away from the easel and toward the house. "How's your paperwork coming? Time for a lemonade break?"

"Remember, the first sign of pain in your wrist, let me know. These get-togethers tend to go on until dawn." He'd parked near a house on the edge of the waterfront and was helping her out of the car as he spoke.

"Alex, you said you haven't seen these people in three months. I'm not about to take you away from them at the first little ol' twinge." Straightening the standaway collar on her dress, she looked down at the pink-cabbage-rose-and-multileaf print, then up at Alex, who was staring at her. He was also drumming his fingers on the roof of the car.

"What's the matter?" She looked down at her dress again and sighed. "Don't tell me there's a dress code for these get-togethers." If there was, she was going to be disappointed. She thought she'd left those rules behind her. "Well, will I do?" she demanded.

He lifted his hand from the roof and twisted it in a helpless gesture. "You look great," he said, his voice strangely husky.

"Oh. What is it, then?"

"I just wanted to tell you, before we go in, that this group can get rowdy."

Widening her eyes, she laughed. "Rowdy? I've never done 'rowdy' before." He had to be joking of course, or exaggerating. Rowdy was a condition reserved for rodeo riders and barroom brawlers. She shook her head as they walked to the house.

As Alex reached for the handle, the door was opened by a tall, bearded man in a kilt. He leaned out and kissed Sandy noisily on both cheeks.

"The last time I saw you, you were curled like a wee kitten in Alexander's arms." The Scotsman slipped a bottle of beer into her hand and wrapped his arm around her, saying to Alex, "You're needed in the kitchen. Taro wants you to taste the sauce."

She twisted to look at Alex, not sure of what she should do.

"Now, lass, unless you're plannin' to catch the midnight plane to Athens, you'll have plenty of time to spend with Alexander. Right now, some of us need a fresh opinion on a subject dear to my heart. My name's Bertram, by the way, and yours is Sandy, but you've known that for years."

She went with him to the piano and, without warning, he picked her up and deposited her on top of it. The group already leaning against it made hasty introductions, and the argument over the fashionable versus the proper length of a man's kilt continued. After reaching a loud impasse, the subject suddenly changed to a fail-safe dysentery cure if one happened to be stranded in southern New Guinea.

The enthusiastic sixsome had her clutching her sides with laughter, and before she realized it, an hour had slipped by. She looked up several times for a glimpse of Alex. Sometimes she caught him looking at her in a way that made her want to straighten her dress or pat her hair. Once when Bertram saw her looking for him, he closed his hand over hers.

"It's good that a man has his space, lass."

She returned the Scot's generous smile, then shook her finger at him. "It's good for a woman too."

Bertram roared his laughter. "Alex," he shouted, "she's a bonny lass. Bonny lass."

Nothing, Sandy soon learned, was considered a taboo subject for the group, but Bertram insisted on withdrawing her from the discussion on goat breeding.

"I'm fifty-eight years old, and I don't want anyone telling me, or our guest here, that goats don't come from acorns. Come along, Sandy," he said, lifting her down from the piano, "I'll give you a look at the gallery before dinner. It's a few doors down, and we'll have ourselves a fine chat along the way."

Dear God, she looked beautiful, Alex thought. Wrapped in roses, scented with honeysuckle, and dripping with southern charm. He caught the shrug she sent his way, then watched as she followed the kilted Scotsman out the door. As boisterous as Bertram was, he had a sensitivity about the moods and feelings of those around him. Alex hadn't had a moment alone with Sandy since they'd walked in, but he was grateful to his friend for getting her outside for a quiet moment. Not that he didn't have enormous admiration and respect for his friends, but their free-spirited antics would never play in her society. No matter that she'd insisted she was ready for a "real" life, ladies like Sandy Patterson flourished much better in their own polished environments.

When dinner was served in the lantern-lit garden, Alex made certain he was seated across from her. He'd seen the way she'd looked for him all throughout the evening. Well, maybe three or four times, if he was honest. Every time he attempted to join her, his friends would corral him back into their group. If he didn't know any better, he'd think there was a concerted effort to keep him away from his houseguest.

Just when he wondered whether she was faking her laughter at still another of Bertram's colorful stories, she joined with two other Americans in singing "The Star-Spangled Banner." Alex whooped with the others at its conclusion, but wondered how she was going to feel about her actions tomorrow. As harmless and good-natured as her performance had been, he knew she wasn't the type to call attention to herself like this.

When he was finally able to slip away from his friends, he spotted Sandy alone in the garden. She stood by one high wall, her posture-perfect, ivory-toned shoulders glowing in the lantern light. Whether it was the flowered dress moving in the breeze or the way she'd gathered her hair high on her head, she gave off an aura of femininity that made his mouth go dry. There was probably a time in the past when knowing she'd belonged to Jackson would have caused Alex to feel guilty about his attraction to her. Fact was, Jackson had been a lucky man, but Jackson was gone now. Alex couldn't muster one guilty feeling to cling to in his effort to fight his desire for her. He shoved his hands in his pockets and wished like hell he'd remembered his cigarettes.

"Well, you're certainly full of surprises."

She looked over the rim of her after-dinner drink, then lowered it to smile at him. Bagpipe music was alternately whining and waning in the house. "Whatever are you talking about? I haven't danced on the piano . . . yet."

"I'm talking about your hobby." He pulled one hand from his pocket and wiggled his finger in the air. "That little sketching thing you do. That knack of yours that got you accepted to one of the most prestigious art schools in America."

"Oh, that little hobby. Who told you?"

"Bertram. He says Chevalier is one of the best schools in the States."

She placed her splinted wrist against the creamiest, roundest cleavage ever to blossom forth from a sweetheart bodice.

"And you're surprised they chose me?"

He looked at anything in the garden that wasn't Sandy. "No. I'm surprised I'm the last to know."

She'd meant to tell him sooner. Pressing the rim of the glass to her lips, she tried looking contrite. It was next to impossible with all the music and laughter coming from inside the house. "Are you throwing me out in the streets for my oversight?"

Before Alex had a chance to reply, someone stopped the bagpipe tape, then started another.

"This one's for Alex's friend, Sandy."

"Georgia on My Mind" wafted out into the garden.

Sandy placed her glass on the window ledge. "Well, bless his heart," she said, holding her hand out to Alex. "Here's a surprise for you. I'm not going to ask you to dance with me on the piano, but I'd love a few turns around this garden. Relax, I've had all my shots and haven't bitten anyone since Thursday." Without waiting for his response, she slipped into his arms.

She felt more than heard his laughter, as he eased her closer and began to dance. Like most men she'd danced with, Alex managed to hold her at a safety shield's distance. Once his fingers brushed the skin above her zipper, and she welcomed the tiny tremors passing between them. When wind swept into the garden and blew a curl of her hair against his hand, he didn't bother to move it. His chin grazed her head twice before he finally gave up and rested it there. The world moved back, spinning silently around them.

After a while he asked, "What were you doing out here all alone?"

"Just studying the silhouette of the church's dome against the streetlight. And giving you time to get reacquainted with your friends."

"That wasn't necessary."

She stopped dancing and looked up from the circle of his arms. "I wanted to."

"I've hardly seen you all night."

"I saw you looking at me."

He danced her slowly around the garden, pressing her body more intimately against his with each turn.

The wind picked up, plastering her skirt against both their legs and that curl of hers against his hand again. He tucked the errant tress behind her ear, then let his thumb slide down her cheek and under her chin. His breath smelled sweet, and she remembered how, when he was eating his dessert, his lips glistened with honey.

Just when she thought he was going to kiss her, someone shut the door. The song diminished to a background whisper, and the intimate moment disappeared.

Alex stopped dancing, took a step backward, and forced himself to cough. "How's your wrist? If you're tired, we could leave."

"Leave? Why? I'm having a fabulous time. Aren't you?"

"Sandy, this isn't exactly your debutante ball at the country club. You don't have to pretend—"

"Oh, Alex," she said, thoroughly exasperated. "I thought we were beyond all that, but you're doing it again."

"What? What am I doing?"

She planted her good hand on her hip and narrowed her eyes. "You're sticking me in a slot. This one's called Country Club Snob."

"I never called you a snob."

"You didn't have to." She gestured with her splinted wrist. "Look, maybe I haven't gotten up on the piano and danced the Highland fling like Bertram, but that doesn't mean I didn't enjoy watching him do it. And did I complain when the octopus salad was served without a fork? As a matter of fact, when you tried to convince me to take off my clothes and go skinny-dipping this morning, I thought I handled that rather well too."

"I'm glad you brought that up," he said, not looking at all glad. "I want to apologize for making you so uncomfortable on the beach this morning. After all, you're—"

"Slot number two."

"You're my friend's widow."

"Is that all you think about when you look at me?"

Looking away from her, he brought both hands to his hips. "I—yes." Nodding vigorously now, he continued emphatically. Too emphatically. "Yes, I see Jackson's widow."

"Alex, that's like me saying, 'Meet my friend, Alex. He's a graduate of Braxton University.' That may be a true statement, but it doesn't tell a tenth of who and what you are." He looked away, but she took him by the sleeve and made him look at her again. "When you look at a rainbow, you don't see only the red part. Right?"

He nodded once, reluctantly.

"Well, when you look at me, why do you see only one part of me?"

"Sandy, we know each other because you are Jackson's widow. I can't forget that."

"Really? I think you've forgotten it a few times," she said evenly, as she placed her hand on his chest. His heart was beating double time.

"And I've said I was wrong. Wrong about the way I talked to you on the beach and wrong about kissing you yesterday. Please accept my apology."

"No, I don't accept your apology." She ran her hand up the front of his shirt, and with a white-knuckled fist gripped the shoulder of his shirt. "If I did, my life would be a rerun of the one I've left behind." She backed him up to a chair and gave him a little push until he sat down. Looming over him, she continued. "And you remember what a summer rerun's like, don't you?"

Moving her face closer to his, she dropped her voice to a threatening softness. "Sterile cubicles filled with polyester people wearing vapid smiles." Sliding her hand over his nape, she let her fingers stray up into his hair. "Where people stand where they're told to stand, where no one dares deviate from the script, and . . ." His face was tipped upward, his mouth was open, and he looked as if he expected her to explode. She had a bigger shock than that in store for him. " . . . where there are no surprises like this."

She lowered her face and, looking into his eyes, kissed him hard on the mouth. She didn't let up on the pressure, but concentrated on the honey-flavored lightning stinging her lips and the surprised expression she saw in his eyes. They widened as her enthusiasm increased.

When he finally realized she wasn't letting up, he pulled her into his lap and deepened the kiss still further.

Four

Once Alex had gathered her into his embrace, she was no longer controlling the kiss. He was. He meant to give what he'd gotten, a stirring lesson on the power of surprise. It would have worked, too, if she hadn't closed her eyes. With that sign of surrender, the challenge vanished, and all he wanted to do was touch her with his lips. Soft, sweet butterfly kisses beginning at her eyelids and ending at her toes. He began trailing those kisses down her cheek, over her throat, and into the velvet hollow of her shoulder. Lingering there was his undoing. Sliding his hands up her rib cage, he rubbed his thumbs over the polished cotton of her bodice and her peaking breasts.

"Ahhh, Sandy," he whispered, bringing her dress below one nipple. He lowered his mouth to stir the rosy peak with his tongue. Each taste deepened his hunger for more. When she cradled his head in both hands and whispered his name, he knew if he didn't stop now, he never would. Releasing her nipple, he eased the material over it and looked up at her. Beneath half-closed lids her gaze still simmered with desire.

She whispered his name again, then opened her eyes. Slowly she eased herself up from his lap. She took the moment with her, leaving him aching for more. *This was not going to happen again.* He leaned his elbows onto his knees and stared straight ahead.

"Alex, it wasn't supposed to go that far."

She wasn't reprimanding, and she wasn't sorry. If anything, she was in awe of what had just happened between them.

"It's okay." He pushed for a friendly smile, and when she tried to match it and failed, he laughed softly. "We'll both survive."

Alex had turned into a tour guide, and it was all her fault.

He'd excused himself from their waterfront table and had gone on an impatient search for the waiter. Today he was taking her on a walking tour of the town. They'd visited a monastery the day after Bertram's party and spent all day yesterday at an archaeological-dig site. If Alex kept this up, she'd need new shoes within the week.

His energetic pace wasn't fooling her; she knew what he was trying to do. He was attempting to erase the memory of the other night in Bertram's garden. She pulled an ice cube from her glass, popped it in her mouth, and smiled. Fat chance of that!

Until Bertram's dinner party she'd believed she could win the battle over her compelling attraction to Alex. His exquisite tenderness had shattered that belief. True, she'd started the crazy kiss, but Alex had been the one to change it to a passionate act of revenge. If he'd ended it there . . . but he hadn't ended it there. He'd kept up those pagan kisses until she thought she would melt in his arms. Then he'd administered the coup de grace, and all her intentions of not losing her heart to Alex Stoner were now paving the road to hell. Or was it heaven? He'd taken her over a threshold to heaven with the ragged whisper of her name and, despite what she had told him, she was never going back.

She rested one arm on the table as she spotted Alex weaving his way through the crowded waterfront restaurant. She wasn't the only one watching his beautifully muscled torso twist and turn through the maze of tables and chairs. Other women turned to look at him, their slow smiles testifying to their appreciation. A few then looked at Sandy, and one even shook her head. The woman's gesture could have meant anything, but Sandy had her own interpretation. *Some kind of wonderful.* She smiled back at the woman as Alex wedged his way between the last of the tables and chairs.

"That took longer than I expected. I finally found our waiter. He was out back kicking around a soccer ball with his friends."

When she looked up, she made certain Alex saw a tiny, knowing smile on her face. *I haven't forgotten that kiss the other night, and neither have you.* "I didn't mind the wait. I can be very patient."

He picked up the bottle of Orangina, took a swallow of the popular soft drink, and set it back on the table. "Ready?"

"Almost." Pulling her sweater from her shoulders, she reached into its pocket and took out her gold chain. "Eleni took this off me the night we arrived, and I haven't been able to put it on because of my wrist. Would you fasten it for me?"

"Sure."

She had to give him credit. He didn't hesitate, and he didn't fumble with the catch. He wasn't as successful hiding his slight gasp when she leaned forward in her chair. Her sleeveless aqua sundress, so schoolgirl modest in the front, dipped halfway down her back. When he'd finished, he stepped in front of her again with his hands already shoved into the pockets of his khaki shorts.

"How about a look at a few jewelry shops? Most of them are just one street up from here," he said, trying to look eager about his proposition.

Standing, she smoothed the front of the barely knee-length dress, then picked up her purse and sweater and tucked them under her splinted arm. Nonchalantly reaching for the soft-drink bottle, she said, "Great. Maybe I can find something for my mother."

His eyes locked onto the bottle as soon as she lifted it. "You didn't leave me much," she said, teasing him as she raised it higher to judge what he'd left. After squinting, she took a swig.

"Was that your drink?" he asked.

As she touched her fingers to her mouth, her eyes opened wide and she nodded. "I think it was. That sort of thing doesn't bother you, does it?" She tilted her head at his startled expression.

Alex stared at her lips again. They were glistening wet and parted. "No," he lied. The hell it didn't bother him. First her mouth, then his, and now hers again.

She might as well have kissed him. No. He didn't mean that, even in jest. Even to himself. He eyed her suspiciously. If he didn't know better, he'd think she was trying to . . . what? Flirt with him? Seduce him? A disturbing sensation shot through his stomach at the thought. Had he been so busy fighting his own attraction to her, he'd been blind to her continuing interest in him? The only way he was going to know for certain, he decided with extreme ambivalence, was by paying more attention to her.

During their walk to the jewelry shops she asked the usual questions about the whitewashed cubist architecture in the town and the shiny blue doors and shutters on all the houses. Their progress was slow because each brightly colored flower or trailing vine had to be looked at, touched, and smelled. Without her verbalizing it, he understood why. She was gathering vacation memories to take back home to share with her friends. He pictured her seated at an impossibly long dining-room table, talking about her trip to Greece. He wondered what she would say about him.

Between the flower stops she talked about the kind of gift she wanted for her mother. He only half listened. He'd redirected his concentration to her body language. The way she gestured with her hand, wrinkled her nose, tossed her hair. *Unaffected* was the only word he could think of—besides *lovely*, *desirable*, and *delightful*—to describe her. Yes, she did manage physical contact with him, but only accidentally, by bumping into him to avoid Petro Theoderakis's donkey. Alex was more confused than ever. Was he imagining subtle flirtations, or was she simply being herself? Patient and confident and natural.

"Alex, how absolutely perfect." She pointed to a ring display in one shop window.

"What is?"

She gave him a playful look of exasperation. "Weren't you listening to what I've been telling you? Mother's birthstone is peridot. The ring on the left, the one designed in the shape of an Omega—see it there? There's a peridot set in the middle."

Twenty minutes later she left the shop with a satisfied smile, and he left knowing her ring size was the same as her mother's, six and a half. He also found out Sandy's birthstone was ruby, but that she preferred the red stones mixed with pearls. Most women had left him notes about this sort of thing, or had others tell him, or simply told him themselves. He'd learned the information about Sandy by listening to her chatty exchange with the jeweler. Not that he planned to do anything with the knowledge of course.

"They'll have the ring sized by next week, and I'll be able to send it to my mother in time for her birthday. Thank you, Alex."

"What are you thanking me for?"

She lost her opportunity to answer him. As they walked along the winding street, a group of picture-taking tourists eventually separated them. While he waited for the shutterbugs to pass, he stared across their heads at Sandy. A blood-red geranium curling up a staircase had caught her attention. She stooped to look into the planter the thick stalk was growing from and then shook her head. When they fell into step again, she grabbed him by the wrist.

"Alex, I have friends in the garden club who would kill to know how to grow geraniums like that. How do these people manage it?"

"We'll ask Eleni." They walked on quietly for a few seconds. "You'll have lots to tell your friends about when you get back."

"I guess I will."

There he was again, thinking about her leaving. He couldn't name the feeling in his gut, but it annoyed him that he experienced it every time he thought about her not being near. "What were you thanking me for a few minutes ago?"

"For waiting until I'd found the perfect gift for my mother. I know most men would rather have a root canal than take a woman shopping."

"Really? How bad is a root canal? I've never had one."

She gave him a soft slug in the shoulder, then walked on with a smile. Surprising to him, watching her try on jewelry had turned out to be an enjoyable pastime. He pictured her sitting at the glass display counter, running her fingers over the rows of rings. As she tried on each selection, her look of concentration mixed with her smiles of approval. At one point she looked up at him and said, "I love buying pretty things for my mother." Her heartfelt comment struck him with a double edge. It was only in recent years that he'd located and begun to reconcile with his own mother. She'd left him and his father when Alex was five. Now, when her birthday or Christmas rolled around, Alex would instruct his secretary to take care of choosing and mailing a gift. He was more than a little envious of Sandy's wholehearted enthusiasm for this sort of shopping chore. "Sandy?"

"Yes?"

"How do you—? Never mind." Was he *losing* it? All these years of silence about his heartache, and he'd just come close to opening his Pandora's box of emotions to Sandy. He closed his eyes for a moment. Sometimes the need to speak choked him, and she made it so easy to talk. Lord, everyone loved to talk to her. Gritting his teeth, he reminded himself he wasn't the jeweler who, a few minutes ago, couldn't keep his mouth shut about his brother's diner in New Jersey.

She slowed down. "Was there something you wanted to ask me about my mother?"

"No."

She glanced at him once or twice, and although she looked interested in knowing what he was going to ask, she let the matter drop. Her easygoing manner mixed with her tactfulness set off an alarm inside him. An undemanding woman? The idea alone was intriguing. That Sandy was one scared the hell out of him.

As they walked out onto the waterfront promenade, she gave him a look of astonishment. "Alex Stoner, how in the world did we end up here? I could have sworn we were headed back to the café, but that's way down there," she said, pointing.

"There isn't a straight street in the town. Each one winds back on another, and most are interconnected with alleys or passageways cutting through to other streets.

"You make this town sound like a board game. Candy Land or Chutes and Ladders." She shook her head. "Learning how to get around must have taken you forever."

"Not really. All you have to remember is that the entire town is tucked onto a hill, and all downhill streets eventually lead to the waterfront. The built-in confusion was planned centuries ago to confuse raiding pirates." He pointed his thumb over his shoulder. "We haven't lost anyone up there yet." He chuckled at her still-doubtful expression. "Sooner or later you'll round a bend and see or hear or smell something familiar." Stepping out of the way, he pointed to the door next to him. "Like this place."

Her doubtful expression was replaced with a gasp and then a smile. "It's Bertram's gallery."

Waving her through the open door, Alex followed her in.

Bertram spotted them immediately and came out from behind his counter. "I thought he was keeping you prisoner up there." Ignoring Alex, he gave Sandy a bear hug and kissed her on the cheek. "What has he been doing to you, lass?"

"Actually he's kept me on a forced march since your party." Sandy looked over her shoulder at Alex and raised her eyebrows. "Haven't you, Alex?"

Alex looked from Sandy to Bertram. "She means she's getting a first-class tour of the island."

"He's right," she agreed. "Day before yesterday we visited the monastery, and yesterday we went to the dig site on the north shore. We're doing the town today, and tomorrow we're going to watch Eleni's family make goat cheese."

"He has you on a full schedule, I see. Well, glad you could take a break and visit me. Have a look on the other side of that wall, Sandy. Those watercolors of the harbor I was telling you about were delivered yesterday."

As the men watched her walk away, Bertram began a series of twitching smiles. "I stand corrected."

Alex's brows rose with suspicion. He didn't feel good about where this was leading. "Corrected?"

"I thought I heard you say you hated having to entertain guests every minute. I must have heard you wrong. Sounds to me now like you'll blister Sandy's feet with all this first-class attention you're giving her."

"She's interested—" he began.

"Aye, laddie," Bertram cut in. "And so are you." Laughing, Bertram walked away from him.

Deciding it was smarter to shut up, Alex headed toward the wrapping counter. When, he wondered, had his interest in Sandy become so obvious? And why was his good friend encouraging him to pursue her? Bertram knew he wasn't interested in a long-term relationship. Bertram also had to know that with a woman like Sandy, a long-term relationship was the only kind to have. Alex strained to hear the conversation around the other side of the portable display wall. With a bagpipe tape playing in the background, he knew it wasn't worth the effort. Much to his chagrin he kept on trying anyway. The best he could make out was an occasional coo from Bertram and a helpless giggle or two from Sandy. When he sensed them ending their discussion, he realized what he would look like to them, standing there staring at the other side of the wall. He quickly picked up the phone and began dialing the first number that came to mind. Halfway through, he realized he was dialing his office in Athens and hurriedly hung up, then called his Zephyros house. When he reached Eleni, he stared dumbly into the phone. After his housekeeper asked for the second time what she could do for him, he asked her what she'd planned on making for dinner.

"Kotopoulo fournou," he repeated. And then, *"Horiatiki salata.* Mmmm. *Loukoumathes."* He said good-bye to his bewildered housekeeper and hung up.

"I mean what I say, Sandy. Bring in what you have. I want verra much to see your work."

"How about next week? I ought to have a couple of things ready by then."

"I look forward to it." Bertram patted her hand, then turned to Alex. "She doesn't need to see goat cheese made. Let her be to do some painting, lad. As for you, you're looking tense. Best you should put your feet up and rest. What's the word you Americans use? Stressed. Aye, you look stressed."

"I just talked to my secretary. We're having trouble with a wool merchant." He turned to Sandy. "Ready?" She followed him as he headed for the door.

"Aye, wool merchant. Those wool merchants can be verra stressing." Bertram pulled on the side of his mustache. "Maybe a nice dinner of chicken and potatoes with a little salad will make you feel better.

Oh, and maybe some crisp honey doughnuts for dessert."

Alex stopped in his tracks, causing Sandy to bump into him. "I'll suggest that menu to Eleni." As he steadied Sandy, he shot a withering look at Bertram. The Scotsman only laughed. He'd obviously overheard Alex's conversation with the housekeeper and was letting him know.

"Watch out for those wool merchants," said Bertram. "They'll pull the wool over your eyes, if you let them."

"Yes, I'll remember that too," Alex replied evenly. He hoped the quirky frown he gave to Bertram conveyed a proper mixture of embarrassment, apology, and final warning to his friend. If not, he would have to deal with him again next week. Next week. The temptations of heaven and hell and root-beer eyes loomed large in his mind as he pictured the next seven days with Sandy.

"Alex, do you mind if we don't see how goat cheese is made?"

"It's been my lifelong dream, but I'll get over it."

"You're joking."

"Yes."

"Maybe Eleni's brother would let us see how it's done after next week."

"I think she could be talked into that. Anyway, Bertram's interested in your paintings, is he?"

She nodded. "Alex, did you know he was an art critic in Glasgow before he chucked that rat race and moved out here?"

"Seems to me he mentioned something about that." The hell he had. Alex had known Bertram for over three years, and the wild Scotsman had never mentioned the fact. Alex led her toward several flokatis displayed by the open door of another waterfront shop. Flipping through the edges of one thick stack, he pushed back the top three and ruffled the fourth.

"I told him about a series of seascapes, and he appeared to be interested. What are you doing to that rug?"

"Checking the grade." He blew on the fur, then crinkled his brow as he looked at the depression left in the pile. "About those seascapes of yours," he said as he continued to check the rug. "Does the series include the painting you wouldn't let me look at?" He twisted his head to face her.

"Yes, but I'll show it to you now if you'd like. It's just when the work's in progress, I can't bear to have anyone look at it." Scratching the side of her face, she lifted her chin in the direction of the stack. "Alex," she whispered, "won't the owner wonder why you're being so rough with his rugs?"

Her sincerity was charming, and it made him want to tease her again. Trying to look guilty, he scanned the area, then leaned close to her ear. "I'm the owner." Her shocked expression soon turned to laughter, and he joined her.

She shook her finger at him. "You *are* a very naughty boy."

He turned back to the rugs, pretending he was still sharing a light moment with her. The fact was, he couldn't look her in the eye once she'd called him a naughty boy. Those words took him right back to Delphi and the moment he'd first kissed her.

Nothing had been the same since then. He cleared his throat. "Did you know we don't kill the sheep to make these rugs? And that they're sold by weight and not size? The heavier the rug, the more valuable it is. If you're interested in getting a few, I'll help you choose. They can be mailed from here, by the way."

"They're all so inviting," she said, running her fingers over the soft white fur. "It makes me want to curl up on one and take a nap."

As he watched her plunge her fingers into the fur, he pictured her not curled up but rather stretched out on the rug . . . wearing rubies and pearls . . . and nothing more. He felt desire tightening low in his belly . . . and lower still. "Well, no need to select them today," he said more brusquely than necessary. She pulled her hand away and smoothed back a few strands of hair.

"Right." Shadowing her eyes with her fingers, she looked at the sun and then the shadows. "Alex?"

He felt himself sinking into those big brown eyes of hers. "You'd like to go back to the house and paint, wouldn't you?"

"Would you mind going back this early?"

Yes, I'd mind if you went back and painted. I'd rather you take your clothes off, don some rubies and pearls, and stretch out on my whitest, thickest Flokati. And when we're through, we'll sleep for days. He swallowed. "Not at all. I've got that work to do for the Grimaldi visit."

"Are they the Grimaldis with the gorgeous decorator catalogs?"

"Yes. And if I close the deal with them, it will open up my biggest market yet." He had to concentrate on the Grimaldis, he told himself, and forget about rubies and pearls—and all the rest of that fantasy.

"You're going to burn."

Sandy looked toward Alex as he finished coming down the beach steps. She tried not to let him hear or see her sigh of relief. "Thank you for wearing your bathing suit."

"Well, as long as you insisted we had to, thank you for wearing that one," he replied, eyeing the pink-and-white floral-print bikini. He plunked down the basket he'd brought with him. "It's a new one, isn't it?"

"Why, yes, it is." Looking down at the expensive suit, she prayed she'd remembered to remove the price tags. "How did you know?"

"Your middle's lighter than the rest of you. You need a good strong sunscreen. It's a different sun here."

"Alex, Zephyros is not in a different solar system. The sun shining over this island is the same one shining over Atlanta. Besides, I can never reach my back."

He was in the middle of unfolding a squat beach chair. "I'll help you with that." Sinking down into the striped canvas, he dropped back his head, closed his eyes, and let the air whoosh out of his lungs. "In just a minute."

Covering her bottom lip with her teeth, she fought back a smile. This last week had been torture for him. As limited as her own sexual experience was, she knew she turned him on. All he had to do was walk into the room she was in, and the tension resonated between them. That he continued to want her gave her the patience to wait him out. He was a sexual time bomb; he couldn't hold out much longer. Sooner or later they were going to make love. Until then she was going to look him straight in the eye and dream about how it was going to be with them. And wonder what held him back.

With the gentle sounds of lapping waves a few yards away, she settled back to watch him. In the less than two weeks they'd been on the island, his tan had darkened beautifully. His already light blond hair had lightened even more, and the contrast with his skin resulted in a devastatingly attractive man.

After a minute he spoke. "Sandy?"

"Uh-huh?"

"You could have been down on this beach a long time ago if you'd only asked me to put on a bathing suit."

Sitting up, she crossed her legs in front of her and began unwinding the elastic bandage on her wrist. Her wrist had become strong enough to do away with the splint several days ago. "I could have, but you've seemed a little tense lately."

"Me?"

"Yes, you. I know how much you enjoy the water. I mean, I've seen how much it relaxes you. I didn't want to intrude."

He resettled his bottom in the striped canvas sling and shrugged. "I should have said something sooner, but I thought you were so keen on painting that you weren't interested in the beach." Turning his head, he opened one eye toward her. "Do you realize you have this secret smile when you're at your canvas?"

She pushed up the wide brim of her fuchsia-colored straw hat, then took it off. During the last week he'd alternated tiptoeing around her with bowling her over with his hijinks and conversations. He was at his adorable best this morning, and she was loving it. "Fungi bunk, Alex Stoner. I'm very serious when I paint."

"Seriously happy," he corrected, shaking his finger at her. "You forget, I've been watching you paint for six days in a row."

"All right, I confess. I'm a seriously happy person, and it's all because of you."

His relaxed grin froze. He turned away from her to search through the basket. "Me?" He tossed a container of suntan cream, and she caught it. "That's a strange thing to say."

She adjusted the middle of her bikini top, then stretched out her legs. Squirting a generous amount into her palm, she began applying the cream. "No, it's not strange. You brought me to this island, introduced me to your friends, showed me around. I'm painting exactly what I want to. And this afternoon I'm taking my work to your friend's gallery. Why shouldn't I be seriously happy? You've been wonderful to me." He didn't answer right away. Stroking the cream on the inside of one thigh, she paid careful attention to covering it thoroughly. So did Alex.

Pulling on a baseball cap, he tried locking his gaze to the horizon. "I don't know. You must miss your friends and your family. I've seen you writing letters and postcards."

"I'm not pining away." She looked up to catch him stealing another look at her body. The slick cream, the hot sun, and his blue-eyed stare swirled together in one long caress. He continued watching as she stroked her hips, but his gaze soon strayed to the triangle of material below her navel. If his gaze were a touch . . . she squeezed her thighs together. This delicious power she was experiencing was doubly potent because they were both pretending it wasn't happening. He was breathing through his mouth now. Excited by the sensual spell she was weaving for them, she drew her fingers across the tops of her thighs and down their sides. "You've made me feel welcome here."

"You are," he murmured, wiping perspiration from his brow.

"I mean, like more than just a guest in your home." This time she dabbed the cream above her strapless bandeau top. Drawing small circles with her fingertips over the swells of her breasts, she smiled over at him. "I feel as if you've taken me into your family."

Suddenly he turned back to the basket, and the spell was broken. He pulled out a small bag of cherries. Selecting the best one to eat appeared to have taken on gigantic importance. "Family? What do you mean?" Holding a cherry by its stem, he pulled the fruit off with his teeth, then fixed his gaze on the horizon.

"Bertram, Eleni and her husband. That foursome that dropped by the other night and some of the others at Bertram's party. They may not be related by blood or marriage, but they've become your family."

He chewed the cherry, then spit the pit across the sand. "I don't think you understand—" he began, searching through the bag for another cherry.

"Oh, yes, I do," she said, gently patting the cream around her sprained wrist and hand. "They love you, care about your happiness, and are there to support you. My family does the same thing, only they tend to go overboard. Does yours fix you up with dates too?"

"They do not." He lifted his gaze from the bag and stared at her for several seconds. "Sandy, I've never been close to what few relatives I do have. I don't think of these people on Zephyros as some sort of a substitute family or pretend that this place has some sort of hold on me. Not the way you think of your family or your place back in Atlanta. What's that smile for?"

Recapping the container, she dropped it in her lap. She reached for a covered elastic and, lifting her hair, worked it into a fluffy ponytail on top of her head. "Alex, you'd like to think you don't need anyone or anything to fill your heart besides your business. I don't believe that. You're too kind, too caring a person."

"I'm not a sentimental man, Sandy. I never was, and I never will be." He closed the bag and tossed it into the basket. Wiping his hands together as if he were ridding them of sand, he looked over at her again. "Now, enough talk about me. Let's get that cream on your back." He drew quick circles with his finger, indicating she should turn around.

The more she stayed away from sentimental observations about his life, the more he relaxed. Favoring her wrist, she started the awkward turn on her towel. One moment he was kneeling out of his chair, and the next he had slipped his arms under hers and was dragging her to her feet.

"Whatever are you doing?"

"Finally getting you into that water," he said, as he scooped her into his arms and began running across the sand with her.

She hardly had time to scream as he jostled her against his chest. "Don't you dare. Alex, put me down. Now!" He waded out until the water was up to her rear and his elbows before letting go. The last thing she said before pinching her nose and going under was, "You're in big trouble!"

After a practically lethal water fight, which he won, he gave up tormenting her and treaded water several yards away from her. "I called Bertram before I came down here. He's expecting us around six."

"That'll work out fine," she said, swimming close to him, then around him several times. He hadn't fooled her. The water fight had been his attempt to break the sexual tension between them, and she meant to stir it up again. "I promised Eleni I'd teach her how to make peach pies this afternoon." She held up one palm to fend off the water he was beginning to splash at her. "Stop that. We can take one with us. Alex, stop that." She made the mistake of splashing him back and spent the next five minutes regretting it.

His playful act lasted through a late lunch, pie baking, and the ride into town. With her canvases carefully stored in the backseat and a peach pie sitting on her lap, Sandy listened as Alex told her about the Grimaldi brothers.

"They have exclusive decorator stores in Beverly Hills, Palm Beach, and places like that. Every summer both men and their wives travel to different parts of the world selecting items for their stores."

"And they're coming to see about your rugs?"

"Yes. I expect them next week."

The peculiar feeling in the pit of her stomach was rapidly expanding. Where had the time gone? Was she really going to leave him in a few days? She said the kinds of things she'd been taught to say, but her heart wasn't in them. "I see. Well, I'm sure I'll have this bandage off my wrist by then. I'll be out of your hair in plenty of time for you to prepare the house for them."

He pulled the car into a parking space behind the gallery and set the brake. "No need to worry. I never bring clients out here. I'll be flying over to Athens to meet with them."

She waited for him to say something about her leaving, but he didn't mention it. Staring at the latticed piecrust, she allowed herself a tiny ray of hope as she thought back over the last week. Even in the sprawling one-story house, he always managed to be close by if not a few feet away from her. The one exception was when she painted. Then he slipped into his study and made his phone calls or went down to the beach for a swim. More often than not, he'd show up with lemonade in mid-morning or drinks in the late afternoon to insist she take a break and join him. With his constant nearness, he still managed to never quite touch her. Yet wrapped in the guise of the patient person she used to be, Sandy had never felt so alive, so ready, so willing to be his lover. She squeezed her eyes closed as that confusing question reared up again. Why hadn't he tried making love to her? What was holding him back? Surely it couldn't still be the fact that she was his friend's widow. Jackson and Alex hadn't seen each other since before her marriage to Jackson, and except for the occasional letter the two men had shown little continuing interest in each other. Alex hadn't mentioned Jackson in days. Come to think of it, since Bertram's party neither had she. With only the smallest bit of guilt, she reminded herself how lovely it had been *not* talking about Jackson.

As Alex unloaded the canvases from the backseat, she looked up and smiled at him. She hadn't imagined the looks he'd given her all week long either; he was giving her one at this very moment. The kind of look that had her feeling powerful and weak all in the same moment. Next week was still a long way from this afternoon. Plans could be changed. Anything could happen by next week. Absolutely anything.

Once they were in the gallery and Alex had carefully leaned the paintings against the wall, he broke off a piece of piecrust and ate it.

"I declare, Alex Stoner, you are the limit. I left two pies in your kitchen, so if you don't mind, this one's for Bertram." Placing the pie on the counter, she turned from Alex, but not before she saw him break off another piece of crust. "Bertram? Would you take this pie before Alex eats it all?"

They waited several seconds before Alex called his name. He licked his thumb. "That's strange. He never leaves this place unattended."

His naughty-boy look disappeared when he held up his hand. "Wait here."

She watched as he made a hasty search of the gallery. "In there?" she asked, pointing to the one door Alex hadn't checked.

"I doubt it," he said, shaking his head. "It's an old storeroom he rarely uses." After a moment he shrugged. "Go ahead."

While she went to the storeroom door, Alex headed toward a side exit. "I'm going over to his house. Maybe he—"

Alex never finished his sentence. "Oh, no! *Alex? Alex,* come quickly!"

Bertram lay beneath a fallen box of scrap lumber and the remains of a brick-and-wood shelf system. His complexion was pale, the gash on the side of his forehead was trickling blood, and he was unconscious. "Alex, his breathing is shallow. His pulse—I can hardly feel any."

Alex swore under his breath as he lifted the bricks and wood from his friend. Without thinking about her wrist, Sandy pitched in.

"Bertram? Hang in there," Alex said. "We'll have you out in a minute." Kneeling beside Sandy, he called Bertram's name again and got no response. "Sandy, we've got to get him out of here."

She grabbed him by the arm. "No. Not until a doctor says it's okay. We don't know if anything's broken. We've got to get a doctor."

Alex sank back on his heels and pulled his hand across his mouth. "We can't. Dr. Constantine is in Athens for the weekend."

"Then we'll have to get another doctor. He's bleeding," she said, feeling frantically for Bertram's pulse again. "Alex, are you listening to me?"

Alex looked grim. "There is no other doctor," he said quietly.

Five

Sandy stared at Alex incredulously. "No other doctor? This is terrible! Then call the hospital."

"Sandy, this isn't Atlanta. We don't have a hospital here."

"Well, what *do* you have?"

He shoved his fingers through his hair. "We have a small clinic."

She swallowed hard and did her best to force back the disbelief distorting her features. She spoke slowly. "If the doctor's in Athens, what about his nurse? We could call his nurse."

"His nurse went with him." Alex's laugh was a mirthless sound in the small storeroom. "They're interviewing other doctors and nurses to increase the staff."

Shaking her head, Sandy lifted Bertram's wrist to check his pulse. "It's still slow, Alex, and look at his face. He's losing his color. I think he's in shock. Can you get me some blankets from his house and . . ."

"And what?"

"I've had a first-aid course. CPR training. And that's it. Alex, start calling the hotels to see if one of

them has a doctor or nurse staying there." Her voice
was low, to the point, and ominously slow. "This is a
head injury."

Alex took a long, slow breath, then dragged a hand
over his mouth again. The possibility that Bertram
might not regain consciousness hit him with stag-
gering strength. Sandy had been right when she'd
said his Zephyros friends had become his family.
At least this man had. Why had it taken him until
this moment to realize it? He felt Sandy's hand on
his shoulder.

"Hurry, Alex."

Five minutes later they'd wrapped Bertram in two
blankets, cleaned and bandaged the cut on his forehead, and checked him for broken bones. Finding
none was the only light in the dark minutes they'd
endured since they'd found him. The thought of
losing Bertram had shaken Alex more than he could
have imagined. The comfort he drew from watching
Sandy tend his friend surprised him too. When she
wasn't feeling for his pulse, she was checking his
pupils. Calling Bertram's name over and over, she
rubbed the insides of his wrists.

Alex pulled the phone into the storeroom. His
stare flitted from Bertram to Sandy while he called
the island's short list of guest houses and hotels.
With each negative reply, his feelings of helpless-
ness grew. He'd learned early in life that to want
something too badly was to ask for disappointment.

At one point Sandy looked up at him, and he
couldn't pretend he didn't see the flicker of fear
in her eyes. Rubbing his forehead, he fought the
weariness creeping over him. He wasn't giving up

"There's one more place. The Hotel Apollo on the opposite side of the island."

Twenty minutes later a young Australian doctor was in the storeroom kneeling beside Bertram. Slumped against the wall, with his fingers pressed to his forehead, Alex answered the doctor's questions along with Sandy.

The usual and universal *hmmmms* were the only sounds the doctor made when he examined Bertram. After an ammonia capsule was crushed under his nostrils, the Scotsman regained consciousness, cursing.

"He appears to have the will to live, if only to see us all into hell by teatime. I reckon with his aching head, he'll be bloody disagreeable for the next few days."

Sandy dropped to her knees again. "Oh, Bertram, you gave us all a terrible scare." She patted him on the shoulder. "You're going to have a headache for a while, but the doctor says you'll be fine."

As the doctor prepared to stitch the gash on Bertram's forehead, he asked Bertram a few questions. When he was done, he turned to Alex and Sandy. "I'll be back to check on him tomorrow, but someone will have to be with him around the clock for the next few days. Does he have any family?"

Alex looked at Sandy and smiled for the first time in hours. "In a manner of speaking."

"We'll stay with him," said Sandy.

The doctor raised his eyebrows. "You two look drained. If you think you'd be able to stay awake—"

"Call Claire Seurat," whispered Bertram. "I think,"

he began, then broke off with a wince, "I think she could be talked into spending the night with me."

"Claire Seurat?" Picturing the quiet, fortyish woman, Alex dropped to his haunches beside his friend. "The owner of the new bookstore next to the travel agency? That Claire Seurat?"

Bertram's devilish smile was answer enough, but he added in a whisper, "Aye, she likes me kilt."

After escorting the concerned bookstore owner to Bertram's bedside and extracting a promise that she'd call Alex for *any reason*, Alex and Sandy drove back to the house in a drizzling rain.

"I remember meeting Claire at Bertram's dinner party. Alex, she's such a gentle soul. Have they been seeing each other for a long time?"

"I don't know. She's had the bookstore here for a few months. Bertram brags, but he isn't the type to kiss and tell names." He shook his head as he drove the car into the circular driveway in front of his house. "I just hope she remembers to call me if she needs any help."

"The doctor saw him. He's going to be fine now. Really. You can relax."

He shook his head as if to clear away his groundless fears. "You're right," he admitted. "I just can't seem to get my mind off him." He looked out the rain-spattered windshield at what was now a downpour. "He's like an uncle."

"What did you say?"

He gave her a sheepish grin. "I said, it looks like we're stuck here for a while."

Her comical sneer quickly turned into a mischievous grin. "You know what your uncle would say, don't you?" With a terrible Scottish accent, she asked, "Where's your sense of adventure?" She unhooked her seat belt and opened her door.

"Are you sure you want to do this?"

"Will the South rise again?"

Her soft southern drawl was all the impetus he needed, but when she bounded from the car with an unladylike whoop, he was twice as quick to follow her. Between the car and the front door, their rush through the rain turned into a shrieking race. Letting her win was a pleasure as he watched her marigold-colored blouse and black linen shorts turn into a clinging second skin. Once inside his house, he slammed the door, hit the light switch, tossed his keys on the table, and took off down the hall after her. She'd already crossed the threshold into her bedroom, and without thinking, he followed her in.

She threw a towel at him, and he missed catching it. "You're out of shape, Stoner," she said, looking at the towel on the floor.

Her giddy, nonsensical remark was an expression of the relief they both were feeling. Bertram was going to be fine, and they were home. Home. He stripped off his wet shirt, leaned back against the door, and watched her wipe the rain from her face. As exhausting as the last hours had been, there was a freshness about her that transcended the tension they'd been floundering in. Home. He was home with Sandy. Warmth flooded him, and he couldn't stop staring at her. She was luminous, and the air around them seemed to crackle. He pushed off the door and took a step toward her. Sandy?"

She lowered the fluffy white terry cloth from her cheek. "Yes?"

As if he'd done it for her a thousand times before, he lifted a corner of the towel and blotted raindrops from her chin. "You were wonderful today. You kept your head. You kept on trying. You never gave up." He looked into her eyes as he lowered the towel. "You never let me give up. I don't know how I'll ever be able to thank you."

She touched her towel to his ear and then the side of his face. "You don't?" The towel slipped from their hands as she cupped the side of his face. "I don't believe you."

"I don't either," he said, slipping his fingers through her damp hair and pulling her face to his. He tasted rain and the wetness of her mouth. "God, you're beautiful," he managed through an onslaught of kisses that left her more breathless than their run from the car.

His hot mouth on her rain-cooled lips seared away the lighthearted moment, replacing it with a lusty enthusiasm that thrilled her. "I thought you'd never touch me," she said in a rushing whisper. She reached her arms around his neck and pressed her beaded nipples against his chest.

He held his breath, then felt the moment dissolving around him. She was right. He was never going to touch her. It wasn't right that he touch her. And he had to stop touching her. Right now. He took her by the shoulders and, with supreme effort, moved her away from him.

"What is it? What's wrong?"

He opened his mouth, then took a trembling

breath before he spoke. "This isn't a good idea."

She blinked in confusion and opened her arms in surprise. "W-why?"

He picked up the towels and placed them on the dresser without looking at her.

"Alex?" she whispered, then brought one hand to her mouth. "It's that I'm Jackson's widow. That's still it, isn't it?" He rolled his tongue inside his cheek but still didn't look at her. "I know we haven't talked about him much, but it's been a long time since he died. I put that part of my life behind me, and I thought you would have—"

He stopped her in mid-sentence. "That's not it." He puffed up his cheeks, then blew out through tightened, thinned lips. Lord, why was he denying it? Yes, it was a definite lie that what bothered him was Sandy being the widow of his friend; but she'd more likely accept that lie than the truth. And the truth was she was a defenseless woman going through some incredible changes. He didn't want her thinking she was in love with him. She was just too vulnerable for a mistake like that. Straddling two worlds, she might think she wanted a wild night with him, but when she woke up in the morning, she'd still be Sandy Patterson. No matter how much he wanted to sink himself inside her and hear her cry out his name, he wasn't going to. Whether she realized it at the moment or not, her life was back in Atlanta. Maybe, he mused, Atlanta *was* in another solar system.

For the longest time she watched and waited. She was ready for him. Ready for him to say to hell with all the reasons not to and then peel off her clothes and make love. After an uncomfortable silence, she walked to the window and pushed back the heavy lace curtains. The rain had stopped in time to reveal a half-moon high on the horizon. It glimmered over the Aegean, but she hardly noticed it. If the problem wasn't that she was Jackson's widow, then what could it be? She stared out the window until her eyes burned. Then a thought struck her. A thought so incongruous, she almost ignored it. In the end she simply asked him. "Do you think I kept Jackson away from you?" He didn't answer right away, and she turned to see if he was still there. He was. Naked to the waist, desirable beyond description, and staring at the empty bed. *Tell me it's not true.*

Looking as if he'd rather not be there, he scratched his eyebrow with his thumbnail. "I guess I do," he said, then turned and left the room.

She went to the door, but before she followed him into the hall, she gripped the doorjamb and stopped. There was no way to make this right. If she told Alex the truth about Jackson, he wouldn't believe her, or worse, he'd believe her and despise her for destroying the image of someone he'd once admired. Either way he would see her as a desperate woman begging him for his attentions. Yes, he'd just kissed her, but only in a moment of jubilant relief. If he'd really meant it, he could have kissed her a thousand times during the last week. She'd certainly given him enough opportunities. She'd been so focused on her own desires, she'd seen only what she had wanted to see. From the first day she'd met him, she'd misread the reason for Alex's interest in her. Closing the door, she leaned against it, bracing herself for the worst wave of humiliation to pass. Then she began searching for the strength to do what had to be done.

Two hours of swimming in a chilly sea left his skin tingling, his blood racing, and his thoughts as jumbled as they were the night before. Be that as it may, he told himself, he still had to face her. Hell, he wanted to and needed to—but what he would say was still a mystery to him. The best way was probably to listen to what she had to say and take it from there. He finished dressing, snapped on his watch, and noted the time. Ten-thirty, and he had yet to hear her up and around.

He found a frowning Eleni in Sandy's bedroom making up the bed. "Where is she?"

Eleni stood up, jamming her hands to her hips. She shrugged with a dramatic flare Alex had never seen before.

"She can't be on the patio painting. It's raining again." He opened his hands. "Where is she?"

Leveling an acid look at him, Eleni drew an envelope from her apron pocket, stepped forward, and slapped it into her employer's palm. "She went away in Marcos's taxi."

"She *what?*" he asked, following his housekeeper from the bedroom and down the hall. "Eleni. When?"

"When you went down to do your swimming."

"What did she say?"

"She said her wrist is all better. She said thank you to me and to give you that." Eleni pointed to the letter in his hand.

He was tearing it open when the phone rang. "That's her," he said, more to himself than to Eleni. Heading to his phone in his office, he called back over his shoulder, "We had a misunderstanding. That's all."

"Good morning," he said calmly, then waited for that soft southern accent to wash over him. Several seconds passed as he sat down in his chair behind the desk.

"Is this Mr. Stoner?"

"Maria?" He wasn't expecting his administrative assistant in his Athens office, and his shocked tone showed it.

"Yes, it is Maria. I'm sorry if this is a bad time to call, but I thought you ought to know immediately."

Although he'd had enough surprises for one morning, things couldn't get much worse. "Go ahead."

"The Grimaldi brothers and their wives are here in your office. They left Spain earlier than scheduled. Mr. Stoner, they're not in a very good mood. One of the wives has lost her luggage in transit, and their hotel isn't prepared for their early arrival. What do you want me to do with them?"

This was the last thing he needed today. Dragging a hand over his face, he opened his eyes to see Eleni lowering a tray of peach pie and coffee in front of him. Her hopeful smile tugged at his heart. His housekeeper had grown fond of Sandy, and when he shook his head, her smile turned to a frown. She set the tray down harder than she had to.

"Mr. Stoner?" It was Maria again. "Did you hear me? What do you want me to do with them?"

"Take them to my place and see that they're comfortable. Then call the airport. Find out what you can bout the lost luggage. I have some things to take are of here, but I'll be over today. Tell the Grimaldis ll be in Athens to take them to dinner tonight. A late inner—say, ten o'clock."

By one o'clock he'd found out several things.

Sandy hadn't left by airplane.

She hadn't taken the ferry, because none had yet rrived.

He couldn't talk to Marcos until much later. Marcos and his taxi had been hired out for a tour.

Sandy *had* picked up the peridot ring from the eweler's.

At one-thirty he went to Bertram's.

"Lovely embroidery on your forehead, friend," said lex.

"Aye, I'm told there'll be a scar." Leaning forward, Bertram pointed to his forehead as he whispered to lex, "Romantic-hero material. Claire told me last ight. Imagine. A bang on the head and I'm more esirable than ever."

Alex laughed halfheartedly. "I see you're feeling etter."

Bertram nodded, easing himself back against his illows. "Aye. Thanks to Claire, and to you and andy."

"She's gone, Bertram."

Bertram shook his head.

"Yes, she is. Early this morning, she left without elling me. I'm going to start phoning the hotels and uest houses. She's not used to traveling alone."

"You make her sound like a puppy that's escaped

into a city street. That doesn't sound like the Sand
I know."

Alex stood up and shoved his hands in his pocket
before he began to pace beside Bertram. "You don
understand. She's going through a lot of change
and she thinks she's ready for . . . things."

"Go on," said Bertram, with an urging tone appar
ent in his voice.

"We had a misunderstanding and. . . . Anyway
I've got to find her by tonight, because I have to catc
the eight o'clock flight to Athens." He turned to loo
Bertram in the eye. "I need to use your phone."

"Sandy's staying at Claire's apartment, Alex."

"*What?*" He flattened one hand against his ow
chest and exhaled until his shoulders drooped. H
closed his eyes, waiting for his heart to slow dow
"Why the hell didn't you tell me that when I walke
in here?"

"You didn't ask."

He opened his eyes a full ten seconds later. "Ho
did she end up at Claire's?"

"She came here to say good-bye. She said th
same thing you just did, that you two had a mis
understanding. I thought that was strange, becaus
you've never had a problem making yourself perfec
ly clear to me or to any of the clan." Bertram tilte
down his chin and waited.

"I let her think something bothered me about he
marriage to Jackson."

"Good Lord, lad. She's been a widow over tw
years."

"I said I *let her think* it bothered me. Look, I don
want to talk about this."

The Scotsman nodded respectfully.

"Bertram, how did you stop her from leaving?"

"I told her the truth, which is what you should have done about whatever's between you two. Anyhow, I strongly suggested she wait a few days to see if I could sell one of her paintings. She seemed hot to leave, but after I told her this island wasn't so small that she'd be running into the likes of you every five minutes, she decided to stay." He leaned his head toward his kitchen door. "Since Claire's been considerate enough to move in for a while, she suggested Sandy take her rooms over the bookstore."

Alex began pushing off the chair. "And Sandy's over there now?"

"Aye. But take some advice from a wiser man, lad. Give yourselves a day or two to let the smoke clear. Now, I can tell by that look in your eyes, you're eager to go over there and get into it again." Bertram shook his head. "Take your eight o'clock flight to Athens. Finish your business and come back in a day or two. You'll both make more sense to each other by then."

Alex looked at the door and then at his friend. His thoughts had been on finding Sandy, not on what he would say to her when he did. Charging over there could possible send her packing again. He patted his shirt in search of his cigarettes. He didn't find any; he hadn't smoked in days. "You say she's planning to stay on for a few days?"

"That's what she told me, and I believe her."

Walking to the door, Alex stopped, frozen with indecision. If he was going to take the chance that a short time apart would somehow make things easier between them, he wanted further assurance that she would be here when he returned. "You have my telephone numbers in Athens. If she looks like she's preparing to leave, you'll call me?"

"You're in good hands, lad. Just like I was yesterday."

A feeling he could only describe as sentimental thickened in his throat. He swallowed slowly.

Six

She'd sold a painting.

Or rather, Bertram had sold the painting. One of her seascapes was now in the possession of a young couple from California. A smile lifted one corner of her mouth as she walked along the twisting walkways of the town. The pinwheel-size thrill she felt every time she thought about her first sale should have been a roller-coaster-size thrill. It wasn't, and she knew why. Like the streets that all wound back onto each other, her thoughts always came back to Alex. They would have been celebrating this sale together if he hadn't blamed her for keeping Jackson away from him. Maybe she should have told him the truth that morning at Delphi. Maybe—

She stopped her uphill climb, leaned against a lime-washed wall, and folded her arms with a sigh. No maybes about it. What she hadn't done didn't count; what she *was* doing did. She was exercising patience. Yes, she'd allowed Bertram to think he'd talked her into staying because of the "grand probability" that a painting would sell. As tempting as that prospect had been, she wasn't kidding herself.

She knew the real reason why she remained on Zephyros the last three days and why she planned to spend more time here. Hope. Hope that she'd see Alex again. Hope that he cared enough about her to seek her out and ask for some explanations. Then and only then would she tell him the truth about Jackson. Meanwhile she had things to do. With her self-respect still intact and her longing for Alex still nipping at her heart, she would go about her life.

Taking a deep breath, she made herself think about the reason for her walk this morning. Knowing that painting another seascape would remind her of Alex, she'd decided to do something else entirely. The town was chock-full of colorful scenes, and she was searching for fresh inspiration. Following a curve in the paved street, she walked through an archway and into a sun-drenched square and a riot of possibilities.

Neon-bright flowers clustered at the bases of staircases and near doorways of the dazzling-white buildings. Around the circular rim of a fountain two school-age girls were begging a third for the privilege of cuddling a gray kitten. On the opposite side of the square two black-clad housewives were enjoying a private joke. Beside them was a produce stand loaded with lemons, eggplants, and leafy greens. The universal themes stirred her creative nature, and she raised her camera from its wrist strap to capture as many of them as she could. She took several candid shots of the girls with the kitten, then gracefully continued to shoot them when they smiled into her lens. Kneeling down for a tight shot of some plentiful purple blossoms, she was already blocking out several canvases in her mind. There was plenty of material to keep her painting for weeks. No wonder Alex came to this island. . . . She lowered the camera until her hands stopped trembling, then walked across the square to the stand.

Holding up her camera, she smiled at the women for permission to take their pictures. Their negative and emphatic gestures told her no. Accepting their answer with a good-natured shrug, she then pointed at the produce on the stand. "Okay?" she asked, nodding.

"Okay," one woman answered.

After filling her remaining frames of film with close-ups, she pointed to the lemons and held up two fingers. Reaching into the pocket of her turquoise shirt, she took out enough drachmas to more than pay for the lemons. It was the least she could do to show her appreciation. She watched with guarded concern as the women filled up two plastic bags with two dozen lemons. Two dozen lemons seemed excessive until she remembered that Eleni brought them into the house that way at least once a week. Feeling like more of a resident of the island than a guest, she nodded. *"Efcharisto,"* she said, trying out the Greek word for "thank you," then took the plastic bags of fruit awkwardly against her middle.

She pressed her lips together firmly, but the first giggle had already left her by the time she walked by the fountain. Twenty-four lemons! As she passed through the archway and out of the square, the children followed her. Suddenly the tiny kitten jumped out of the girl's arms and into Sandy's path. Arching its back, it sent Sandy into a fit of laughter when it hissed with the vehemence of a mountain lion. It was the first time she'd laughed at anything since she'd left Alex, and giving into the giddy feeling felt wonderful.

Then it happened. One of her bags lost its twist tie, and a lemon threatened to slip over the top edge. As she tried stopping it with her chin, several more moved dangerously close to it, and then Sandy watched as, one by one, the lemons dribbled over the top and onto the pavement. She bent over to scoop them up. A few seconds later she was holding two empty bags and watching twenty-four lemons scattering downhill.

The three children, along with several shop owners, joined her in the chase. Easter-egg rolls had never been this much fun, she thought, as the walled street echoed with laughter.

When the lemons were sitting safely on a stairway and she'd gotten to practice her Greek "thank you" several more times, she sat down on a step and reloaded the first bag. Halfway through the second, a masculine hand appeared at eye level offering her another lemon. Were people still gathering up fruit? she wondered merrily. "More?" As she began reaching for it, he spoke.

"One more."

Her hand stopped in midair at the sound of his voice. She could hear her heart rattling against her rib cage. Alex. Gorgeous golden Alex in a soft blue shirt and khaki trousers. The moment pulsed with promise. Say something else, she begged silently. *Say something or I'll make a complete fool of myself.*

"I heard you're staying at Claire's." He dropped the last lemon into the bag when she wouldn't take it from his hand.

Breaking her death grip on the plastic, she reached for the second twist tie. "That's right." *Ask me about Jackson. Ask me why he stopped writing.* Stealing a glance at him, she quickly ducked her head to fiddle with the twist tie. She had to stop looking at him. It was bad enough that she was trembling. He didn't need to see the hope burning in her eyes too.

He offered his hand, but she pretended not to see it and pushed up without his help. The uncomfortable silence grew to a tortuous length. In an effort not to betray herself with a further glance, she waved and smiled at the shopkeeper across the road.

Alex glanced behind him, then cleared his throat. "So, Bertram tells me he's sold one of your seascapes. Congratulations."

She nodded, then picked up one of the bags. Silence returned with a vengeance in the lemon-scented air. She ached all over to be in his arms, molding her body to his, feeling his mouth on hers. All he had to do was reach out.

He shifted his weight from one leg to the other and began rubbing the back of his neck.

"Sandy . . . ?"

She stared at her sneakers and held her breath. *Just ask me why.* "Yes?"

"Well, you keep a tight hold on those lemons, then."

That was all he had to say to her? Keep a tight hold on those lemons! Three days of separation, and that's all he could come up with? She felt the anger rising in her chest. She'd just been through thirty-six hours of guilt, pain, hope, and humiliation, and he was telling her to be careful with a couple of bags of lemons. She felt like throwing them at him one by one. Reaching down, she picked up her camera and the second bag. "Say hello to Eleni for me." Tossing her hair away from her face, she started off down the hill.

"I will." He turned to watch the feminine curves of her hips and her slim legs moving seductively beneath her long turquoise T-shirt and tight white leggings. He kept on watching until she disappeared down the hill, and then he slumped against the wall.

After three nights in Athens he thought he'd figured out what he was going to say to her. What he hadn't figured on was her attitude. All along he'd been picturing her the way he'd known her best—relaxed, smiling, and totally engaging. Now she wasn't bothering to look him in the eye. She was so busy with those damn lemons, and waving and smiling at the shopkeeper, that she hardly looked at him at all. He slid down the wall on his haunches. He was simply going to have to wait until she came to talk to him. What was happening to his relaxing vacation? What was happening to him?

"You hate it."

"Hate it? Sandy, are ye mad, lass? It's some of your finest work. Can ye not feel the energy bursting from it?" Bertram took another step back from the painting of eight lemons in a red-striped bowl. "This is a whole new direction for you, and I pray that you pursue it."

She scratched her head as a slow smile spread across her face. "You embarrass me with your compliments."

He waved off her remark as he looked at the two other paintings she'd brought him. "Most impressive. The brushstrokes are bold, adventurous, almost wild, but not so much as to be out of control." He nodded, as they walked to the door. "Aye, lass. You've a bright future ahead."

They looked out at the harbor as the Athens ferry moved into dock.

"I think I won't have the pleasure of looking at your paintings much longer."

"Why?"

"Because someone on that ferry will see them and want to take them away."

"Thank you, Bertram. Thank you for saying the right things." She bit her lip. "I'm grateful you and Claire convinced me to stay." She looked out at the ferry again. "You were wrong about me not running into Alex, though. He stopped and talked to me last week when I was out taking pictures. Since then our paths have crossed several times." She slapped the flat of her hand against the wall. "Damn him! He kept turning up everywhere I went last week. And all he did was look at me, like he expected *me* to say something!" She twisted a lock of hair behind her ear and shrugged. "Maybe it was a coincidence we kept bumping into each other. Anyway, I haven't seen him for two days now."

"He had to go back to Athens, lass. He's been wanting the Grimaldi brothers' business for a long time, or he wouldn't have left." Bertram shook his head as his thoughts appeared to move to another subject. "Look at that steady stream of young day trippers coming off the ferry, will you? A party crowd, I'd say. You won't have a quiet moment to paint if you stay in town today."

"You're right," she said, tamping down her flaring emotions with a sigh. "I've been planning a hike in the hills beyond town. I think I'll do it this afternoon."

"Hmmm. You might consider instead catching the two o'clock boat in front of Spiro's Travel Agency. It's a pleasant ride around the west side of the island to the olive groves near the Apollo Hotel. A charming place for walking and thinking."

Working her way through the crowded waterfront promenade, Sandy reached the boat dock in plenty of time to buy her ticket. The people milling around were in an especially festive mood. Or perhaps she saw them that way because she was in anything but. Alex had been on her mind since her conversation with Bertram.

Alex was playing mind games—mind games he seemed to be winning, or at least scoring well at. She was bothered when he was around, and even more bothered when he wasn't!

Noticing the boat tied up to the dock, she couldn't help but smile. The colorfully painted vessel resembled a child's handmade toy right down to the little red ladder attached to its side. As she fell into line to board, she began to see the possibility of a relaxing afternoon. There was a good deal of laughing and teasing going on in at least four different languages. An atmosphere of contagious fun surrounded her, and she took the opportunity to breathe in the sun-washed sea air. Maybe, for just one afternoon, she could set aside the turmoil in her mind.

"Are you sure you want to take this boat?"

She turned at the first sound of his voice. With her heart filling her throat, she swallowed hard. Her speech still had a breathless quality to it. "Alex."

"You remembered my name."

His sexy smile was not going to seduce her into lighthearted bantering. Neither were his eyes, she decided, as she forced herself to fight them and the other magnetic qualities reaching out to her. Lifting her chin, she turned to face forward in line. "Why shouldn't I take this boat?"

"Do you know where it's going?"

"Of course I know where it's going."

"Well, you've become quite the adventurer."

"Yes, I have."

"Call me crazy, Sandy, but I could have sworn you weren't the type to, uh, commune with nature."

She smiled over her shoulder at him. "You're crazy."

As he paid the ticket seller, Sandy sneaked a peek at her watch. Two o'clock, just as Bertram had said. Of course the Greek lettering on the pink ticket in her hand could have said anything, but she had no reason to doubt Bertram. Still, Alex was chuckling to himself as he stepped into line behind her. She felt herself frowning with suspicion.

She turned her head around. "Are you taking this boat just to follow me?"

"Am I?"

That was the last straw. Determined not to say another word to him, she climbed onto the boat and took an empty place for herself at the rail. Alex managed to maneuver into a space several people down from her. The two pretty Scandinavian girls standing on either side of him immediately engaged him in conversation. In French if she wasn't mistaken. Not wanting to be caught staring, Sandy turned her attention to the passing shoreline. Some relaxing adventure this was turning out to be!

For the next fifteen minutes she tried focusing on the hills and shoreline moving past them. It was next to impossible not to look toward Alex every once in a while. At one point she pulled her sunglasses from her hip bag and shoved them on. If she heard those shrieking giggles from his new friends one more time, she was going to scream.

The good-looking man to her left nodded and grinned at her. "Excuse me. Have you taken this trip before?"

Sandy looked to her right and noticed Alex's attention still riveted to the girls. "Actually I haven't," she answered, turning back. "I hear it's quite lovely."

"I'm Marty Winslow, by the way. I'm from Denver." He offered his hand and an amiable grin.

"Sandy Patterson. Atlanta." Marty seemed pleasant enough, and if Alex happened to take his eyes off those two willowy blondes, he might see she was having a perfectly delightful boat ride herself.

Marty leaned his back against the rail. "I'm mighty

glad you're going to be around this afternoon. Maybe we could spend some time together—"

"Maybe not," said an all-too-familiar voice.

Pushing off the rail, Sandy squared her shoulders and twisted toward Alex. The boat began a sudden turn around a spit of land. The movement threw her off balance, pitching her against Alex. Impact with the muscular wall of his chest pushed her glasses from one ear and left them dangling from her nose. With his hands closing around her, her need for him came back in one sudden rush of desire. The physical reality of his presence was overwhelming, and she suddenly realized how very much she had missed him.

Marty's voice brought her back to reality.

"I think that's up to Sandy."

"I think you ought to mind your own business, buddy."

Sandy straightened her sunglasses and smoothed the front of her top. "Just what do you think you're doing, Alex?"

"Trust me on this, Sandy. You're making a mistake."

Alex hadn't let go of her arm and was continuing to stare at her. The boat's motor lowered to a purr, and all around them people were picking up their bags and heading for the ladder. She could hear the laughter and splashes as people climbed over the side and down into the knee-deep water, then waded into shore.

"Excuse me, Alex, but I don't think I am making a mistake. And if I were, it would be my mistake, wouldn't it?" She pushed his hand from her arm, rolled the hems of her baggy blue pants above her knees, took off her shoes, and headed for the ladder. What had gotten into him? His overprotective manner had more than irritated her once she'd pulled out of that sensual haze he'd had her in. She glanced up at him as she stepped from the ladder into the warm sea.

"I'm right behind you," Alex shouted as Marty took her elbow to steady her against the gentle waves.

Ignoring Alex, she gave Marty an embarrassed smile. "What can I say?"

"I take it you're not seeing each other anymore."

They walked along the shore with the small crowd toward a refreshment stand. "That explains it, more or less. But I still can't imagine what's gotten into him. I didn't think he was the type to make a public fuss," she said, giving Alex a dirty look.

"He probably wishes he hadn't come," said Marty as they walked around the stand.

Sandy tilted her head in confusion as Marty stripped off his T-shirt. "Why do you say that?"

"Too much competition, I expect," he said good-naturedly as he pointed down the beach.

As her gaze followed the direction of his finger, her smile left her lips. At least fifty nude sunbathers were stretched out and relaxing in the sun. She blinked to make certain she wasn't hallucinating, then quickly turned back to Marty when she realized she wasn't. "Oh, my goodness. This isn't the way to the olive groves," she said, tearing off her sunglasses.

Marty wrinkled his nose and shook his head. "Uh-uh. So let's get with the program," he said, unzipping his jeans. "Come on, you can do it."

Alex, accompanied by the Scandinavian girls, walked up to Sandy and stopped. By his amused expression Sandy knew he'd heard Marty's last statement.

Even though she couldn't stop the maddening rush of heat to her face, the rest of her was all strength, dignity, and self-control. "Of course I can do it. I simply choose not to." Hugging her shoes to her breast, she felt her cropped white top ride up in front and expose her midriff. Quickly grabbing its hem, she yanked it down as she attempted unsuccessfully to cover the line of flesh above her waistband. Alex hadn't missed a move. Turning to Marty, she nodded politely. "It was so nice meeting you, Marty. If you'll excuse me, I really have to run now."

Walking around the two blondes, she kept her gaze level as she headed back down the shoreline. She was going to get on that boat, ride it back to town, and never make a mistake like this again as long as she lived. Looking up, she stopped dead in her tracks. Where was the boat? At the same time she spotted it disappearing around the spit, Alex caught up with her.

"Our new friends have decided to join forces for the afternoon. He doesn't speak French, and they don't speak English."

"I'm sure they'll think of some way to communicate," she said, slowing long enough for him to pass her. Veering to the right, she walked away from Alex and the water.

"Wait up," he called after her.

"No." She stopped long enough to slip into her shoes, and then she was off again. But not for long. His hands were on her shoulders, holding her still. Holding her near. Holding her.

"Sandy, we've got to talk," he whispered.

"I can't." She turned to look up at him. "Not here."

He glanced back at the nude sunbathers. "Okay."

Leaving the shore, she followed behind him along a short path that led through a field of blue flowers and out onto a dusty one-lane road.

"There's an old goatherd's shed up the way. There'll be shade on one side. We can sit and talk there."

Several minutes later they left the road and sat down with their backs against the stone shed.

The moment she'd been waiting for had arrived, and she had no idea where to begin. She reached from their shadowed spot into the sunlight to tug at a small green plant. Suddenly the warm air was pungent with the scent of thyme. "Sounds like you know your way around this part of the island."

He laughed quietly. "Yes. As a matter of fact I've been here a few times. Does the public-nudity thing still bother you?"

"No. Yes." She looked at him briefly. "You didn't follow me to ask me that, did you?"

The humor left his eyes. "No, that's not why. We need to talk about other things. Things I should have asked about weeks ago."

She pulled another piece off the plant and crushed it between her palms. "Yes?"

"Jackson's death, his dying, must have been difficult for you."

She'd expected questions about Jackson's life, not his death. "I managed." She looked across the road to a pasture dotted with blue flowers and goats.

Had she resented his remark? Or the way he'd been staring at her? She was sending conflicting messages, but he was determined to sort them out.

"What was it like?"

Pulling her knees to her chest, she leaned her head against the stones and sighed deeply. "He was very businesslike about it. When the treatments didn't work and he knew he was going to die, he decided to take charge of his . . . he called it his closure."

Alex's eyebrows came together in an expression of disbelief. "His closure?"

"That was his way of dealing with his death: turning at least a part of it into something manageable. Controllable. Name it, slot it, deal with it." She gave Alex a sad smile. "You remember Jackson. He always insisted there was a right way and a wrong way to do things. Even to the way a person died. He insisted he was going to die in his grandfather's bed, so against doctor's orders I brought him home. Right up until the end he was busy dealing with his 'closure.' Business, financial, and social." *But not me. He didn't deal with me.*

In the shadows she could see Alex's cool blue eyes beginning to warm with a compassion so real, her heart ached. Could he understand the kind of loneliness she'd felt in those last weeks? Was it possible he'd known an empty space in his own life? She flicked away the pieces of thyme and squeezed her eyes shut. Or was that pity she saw in his expression?

"Sandy, I didn't—"

Speaking quickly, she cut him off. "You think I did or said something to keep Jackson and you apart. Alex, Jackson's one big fling in life was his four years at Braxton University. When that was over, he had satisfied his need for something different. For adventure. I'm sorry if that hurts you, but I'm not going to do to you what Jackson and others have done to me. I'm not going to protect you from the truth. And the truth is, if you didn't belong to his clubs, if you weren't rooted in at least six generations of Atlanta history, if you didn't have old money, if you weren't one of the good old boys, you didn't count."

She watched him for some sign that she'd hit a nerve. He only watched her back.

"Go on."

"In his own way I'm certain he treasured his memories of you. When you were a part of his life, you were an inspiration to him. He admired qualities in you that he didn't possess. I once heard Jackson say, 'Alex Stoner was never afraid to try something new.'" She stood up and walked a few feet into the sunlight.

"After he died, I went through his address book and wrote notes to everybody, including you, who I thought would want to know about his death." She looked across to the pasture again. Several goats looked back, chewing methodically. "He'd saved all your letters. He kept them in a trunk in the attic. The same trunk he kept his college things in. I just found them a few months ago. I could tell by the last few that he hadn't been answering them."

Alex frowned and nodded. When the hell had he

sent those letters? It had been so long ago. "I guess he was too sick to answer them by then." When she didn't answer, he stood up and walked toward her. "Sandy, I'm sorry I'm bringing back these painful memories. I shouldn't have—"

She stepped back before he could touch her. "He wasn't too sick to answer your letters. He'd received them before he was even diagnosed."

She rubbed her forehead, then looked at Alex. He appeared puzzled, but not upset. Not hurt, as she'd expected. "Maybe he wanted to tuck you safely away in his memories where you wouldn't tempt him to . . . examine his own life and the way he was living it. Alex, you were once very important to him. At a time in his life when he could have chosen a different path, you were already stretching your wings. Once college was behind him, he made his choice to live in a way he could . . . manage."

He twisted away to look back down the road they'd come. She stared at the broad set of his shoulders and the way his hair at his nape had peaked with perspiration from the heat. She licked her lips, hoping futilely that her voice wouldn't tremble. "What else did you want to know about Jackson?"

He turned so she could see him in profile. "It was you I wanted to know about. I wanted to know how you'd dealt with his death. How you got through it. How—"

"Alex, I didn't keep Jackson away from you."

He turned fully around to face her. "I never thought you did."

She stared at him for a few seconds. "But—"

He shook his head. "But nothing. Sandy, I was

grasping at straws. I wasn't being honest when I said that I believed you ruined my friendship with Jackson. I was using that excuse to keep us out of bed."

His last statement stunned her, and she felt herself stiffen. "If you didn't want to . . . be with me, why didn't you just say it? I would have left Zephyros days ago, and saved myself this humiliation. Damn you, why did you bother to lie?" Before he could answer, she turned on her heel and walked out onto the road. She could hear him coming behind her, and quickened her pace. But not enough. He took her by the shoulders and pulled her back against him.

She tried to draw away, but he held her fast. "I didn't want us to end up in each other's arms, only to find out that you regretted it all the next morning. Sandy, you're standing on the threshold of the rest of your life. So much is happening to you. You've got art school coming up. Your family's waiting for you back in the States. You're in the midst of this incredible period of self-discovery, when everything seems possible. But, Sandy, you're still the same person when it comes to your beliefs and values and traditions. I just don't want to see you hurt."

He lowered one hand, and she turned to gaze up into his eyes. For a moment the world consisted of one long hungry look. A wrenching look that stripped her bare, titillated her with its heat, and begged her for completion. Then he let go of her and moved away.

"You might think you can handle this electricity buzzing between us, but I think you'd be setting yourself up for the biggest mistake of your life. I'm not the kind of man who's looking for happily-ever-after. When you awakened in the morning, you'd find out that that's exactly the kind of person you still are."

She heard the words, but they were meaningless to her. Meaningless because she was already facing the real and undeniable truth. And it was all there in Alex's eyes. He might believe he was keeping his distance because he didn't want to hurt her. He might think he was being noble and brave, protecting her from a big mistake, but that wasn't it at all. Alex Stoner *was* afraid to try something new. Of taking a plunge into "ever after." Of loving and being loved.

Then another astonishing truth hit her. Whether he realized it or not, he was already in love with her.

And she was in love with him.

Her love for Alex Stoner filled her heart like the sunlight filling the fields around them. And suddenly everything was possible. On a dusty road by a field of blue flowers and bearded goats and a tumble-down shed, she made a silent promise to him. *Before this summer ends, I'll take your fear away.*

"Sandy, do you understand why I did what I did? Can you accept that I was concerned about you and your future?"

His look was incredulous, and with good reason. She was standing in the middle of the road smiling at him. Forcing a serious look onto her face, she pressed her lips together and nodded. "I do. I understand what you're saying and why you're saying it." She kept on nodding, unable to think of what to say next.

He began nodding too. "Well, good. I'm—I'm glad you do." Studying her and still nodding, he narrowed his gaze. "You're sure?"

"Oh, yes. Absolutely." She was beginning to feel like a puppet and abruptly stopped her nodding. Instead she opened her hands, palms up. "So, where do we go from here?"

"Where do we go from here?" he repeated.

It was obvious he hadn't planned this part of the conversation and was now at a loss as to what to say. Not many people, she supposed, had ever seen this in-charge man so bewildered. He'd thought he was going to have more of a problem convincing her than he had, and when it hadn't turned out that way, he was terribly confused. She fought the smile creeping up her face. As much as she'd love to, she was not going to hug him.

Clearing her throat, she made a show of looking around. "Yes. Where do we go from here? Do we go back that way and wait for another boat?" she asked, pointing behind him, "Or is there a bus we can catch up this road? We really do need to get back to town and—"

"Oh, great!" he said, shoving his fingers through his hair. "The Grimaldis. I forgot all about the Grimaldis."

"Where are they?"

"I'm not sure."

"Alex, you sound like you misplaced them."

He took her hand, and together they started to run up the road. "In a way I did. I left them wandering the waterfront."

andy's calm acceptance of his reasons for not making love had him vaguely suspicious. He'd expected an argument or at least a debate. She had certainly taken it well and *appeared* to have put the discussion out of her mind. He looked at her again as she helped him search the harbor town. His flicker of suspicion was dampened by her apparently sincere interest in finding the misplaced Grimaldis. It was as if the revelations of the last two hours had never occurred. That was the last thing he would have expected from someone who, less than two weeks ago, responded so richly to his kisses. Who tasted and smelled like warm honey. Who had him not just looking at her—

"What kind of mood were they in when you left them?" Sandy asked.

"Were who in?"

She laughed in that way that caused a warm, curling sensation in his chest. Was that sparkle in her eyes always there, or did it have something to do with the reflection from the harbor? He blinked, then looked at the sugar-white Cycladic houses on the hill behind her. "Oh, the Grimaldis. Not a happy mood. I thought if I got them out to Zephyros for few days, they might loosen up and begin to enjoy themselves." He scanned the promenade so that he didn't have to look her in the eyes and risk losing his mind. "That's not entirely true. I needed to talk to you, and I haven't closed the deal with them yet, so I convinced them to come here for a couple of days instead of taking the ferry to Mykonos." Removing his sunglasses, he pinched the bridge of his nose and laughed. "I think they'd have been better off going on to Mykonos." He looked toward the empty space at the ferry dock, then sat down on a bench against the whitewashed wall. "Maybe they *have* gone to Mykonos."

"They're here somewhere," she said reassuringly. "But why would you say they'd be better off going to Mykonos?" Unzipping her hip pouch, she busily searched through it while she waited for his reply.

"Because Eleni's over there at her niece's wedding and won't be back until next week. I'd left the Grimaldis drinking ouzo at this *taverna* so that could see about hiring another cook, and . . ."

"And?"

She placed an amber-colored barrette between her teeth and was smoothing her hair into a sleek ponytail as she looked at the fishing boats.

"And then I saw you." *And I couldn't think of anything but you.*

She didn't appear to be listening, and when she looked at him again, she threw her arms open in a gesture of surprise. "Oh, Alex. What fools we are. Think a minute," she said, pulling him from the bench and leading him down the promenade.

"The Grimaldis are here looking for items for their shops and catalog. Besides your rug shop, where else would they be?"

Together they pointed at each other. "Bertram's!"

"She's a new talent I'm pr-r-roud to represent, Mrs. Grimaldi," they heard Bertram saying as they entered the gallery. "An American artist capturing the essence of Greece, and with such a fresh and provocative style." Bertram stuck his head around the portable display wall at the sound of their entry. "Would you look at that," he said, with his back to the Grimaldis. "Here's the very one I'm speaking of, Miss Sandy Patterson of Atlanta, and she's with your host." Bertram's wink was exaggerated to the point of looking like it came from a vaudeville comedy routine.

While Alex scrambled for an acceptable excuse for abandoning them, the Grimaldis appeared from behind the wall.

"You must think we're terrible, leaving that waterside restaurant without waiting for you. And we've been gone almost two hours." Caroline Grimaldi turned toward her relatives. "Poor Alex has probably been frantic looking for us. Haven't you, Alex?"

Frantic? What an articulate woman, he thought dryly. "I don't want you to give it another thought," he said, waving off her concern.

When the introductions had been made, the Grimaldis drew Sandy to the display, and Bertram took Alex aside. "So, you found her?"

He wanted to explain what had happened, but

held back because of his own now-confused feelings. "She took the other two o'clock boat."

Bertram roared with laughter.

Alex couldn't help smiling. "It's a long story."

His Scottish friend stared at him without restraint, then nodded slowly. "And would this long story still not have an ending?"

Alex rubbed his mouth as he searched for words to satisfy Bertram . . . and himself. To his own consternation, he was becoming more confused than ever about Sandy. Since he'd told her making love was out of the question and since she'd accepted what he'd said, he couldn't keep his mind on anything else. As if it were bad-tasting medicine, he kept trying to swallow what had transpired by the goat shed. A sense of well-being continued to elude him. What the hell was wrong with him?

Sandy's laughter floated through the gallery, and he felt his stomach contract with the sheer force of wanting her. He couldn't take his eyes from her shoes, visible below the display wall. She'd poised one foot on its toes slightly behind the other. The position reminded him of the way she stood at her easel, and the memory made him ache. "They like her paintings?"

"Aye. They're mighty impressed. As they should be."

Alex nodded, then turned back to his friend. Bertram was smiling one of his all-knowing I-told-you-so smiles. Alex cleared his throat, making sure that he sounded like his old self. "Before I forget, where can I find a cook for the next day or so?"

Bertram shook his head slowly as they walked

over to the others. "You've got me there. Every-one I'm thinking of has gone to Mykonos for that wedding."

"Alex, there you are. I was just telling Caroline and Beth I've been ordering my personal stationery through their catalogs for years."

Alex barely heard Sandy. He was staring at her paintings. Colors exploded from the canvases, capturing the attention of anyone with a working pair of eyes. He turned to Sandy. "They're remarkable. Truly remarkable," he said quietly as he tried to come to terms with his feelings. These new paintings had an intensity that shook him. What else, he wondered, didn't he know about Sandy Patterson? What other changes was she capable of? And what was it about her confident smile that had him quaking in his sneakers?

He was staring into Sandy's eyes when one of the Grimaldi brothers spoke. "I agree, Stoner. Especially the lemons in the red-striped bowl. Would you mind if we invited Sandy to dinner?"

"Dinner?" Alex repeated. He still hadn't found a cook, and since all he could manage were tuna-fish sandwiches and canned soup, things were looking dismal again.

"I guess Alex didn't have a chance to tell you," said Sandy as she stepped forward and took Alex by the arm. "I am coming to dinner. As a matter of fact, I'm cooking it."

"Sandy, we haven't had barbecued chicken since we left the States. And that fried okra was such a treat. I haven't had any since I was a girl back in Arkansas." Caroline Grimaldi placed two more dishes onto Alex's counter.

"Are you sure you won't let us help you with these?" Beth Grimaldi asked.

"Absolutely not," insisted Sandy. "Alex brought you all out to Zephyros to relax."

Handing the woman a tray of ouzo, glasses, water and ice, he said, "If you'll take this out onto the patio we'll finish up in here and join you in a few minutes." Once Caroline and Beth had left, Alex turned back to Sandy, shaking his head. He would have loved to sweep her into his arms, sudsy hands and all, but he'd done away with that sort of possibility with his talk earlier in the day. He settled for moving closer to her as she squirted more liquid soap into the sink. "You saved my butt tonight."

Her deadpan look alarmed him at first.

"I know." She winked in the same outrageous manner Bertram had.

Then it occurred to him just how much he'd missed her sense of humor. He moved restlessly against the counter's edge. Was there a hint of intimate exchange evident in her look, or was he only desperately searching for it? He picked up the rubber scraper and began scraping the food into the trash.

"I mean it, Sandy. I don't know what I would have done if you hadn't jumped in."

She shrugged. "You would have taken them to the *taverna* in town. The food's good, and the ambience is charming there."

"It wouldn't have been the same. You held them spellbound during dinner."

"Spellbound? Alex, I wouldn't say I held them spellbound."

You held me spellbound. "Whatever—anyway, they've been having a wonderful time since meeting you." He leaned closer again and lowered his voice. "I've been working on this account for over a year, and bringing them here without planning it was a real risk."

She broke their stare as she lifted the stack of plates into the sink. "Alex, Alex, Alex. Everything's a risk." She shrugged dramatically. "Serving fried okra to virtual strangers was a risk," she added, attempting to lighten the moment between them.

Alex laughed quietly. "You're not going to let me thank you."

"Not tonight," she said, dabbing the end of his chin with soapsuds. "We're having too much fun for such sober gratitude," she added playfully.

He closed both hands over hers and felt as if a magnetic current passed between them. "It isn't just gratitude."

"Hey, you two."

Joe Grimaldi had stuck his head into the kitchen. "Come on out here. We have an idea we'd like to run by you."

"Go on, Alex, I'll finish up here," Sandy urged.

"We want you both," insisted Joe.

A few minutes later Alex and Sandy joined the foursome by the patio rail overlooking the Aegean. The tiki torches still flickered from dinner, casting a festive light around everyone. Joe Grimaldi poured them each an ouzo and water.

"We need to know if you two would be interested in our idea."

Alex looked at Sandy, then raised his brows in unabashed interest. "We're listening."

"We're ready to sign for your flokatis, by the way," Joe told him. "But what we want to discuss is something else. Caroline and Beth remembered seeing a small display of hand-tufted rugs in your Athens office."

Alex set his glass of ouzo on the table. "Yes. Pure wool ones. We sell them, but because of the cost and the limited call for them, it's a sideline we haven't aggressively pursued."

Joe Grimaldi looked at his brother, Rigo, who stepped forward. "Our wives, like ourselves, are quite taken with Sandy's paintings. With a little assistance from the computer, the pictures can be woven into area rugs and wall hangings." Rigo turned to Sandy. "We could offer them in our catalogs along with a limited-edition print of your paintings."

"The lemons in the bowl would be our first choice," continued Caroline. "Those bold red stripes curving in one corner of a rug would be fabulous." Closing her eyes and shaking her head, the woman was soon lost in her own musings.

Trying to contain her own excitement over the proposal, Beth picked up the slack. "We don't want to rush you, but Rigo said next summer's catalog will be featuring the Stoner flokatis. I think it would be a wonderful idea to be able to offer the art rugs too."

Alex had been watching Sandy's reaction to the new idea. She seemed to shut down for a few moments, and her eyes took on a glazed, blank look. She nibbled her lip while she concentrated on the excited talk among the Grimaldis. The four family members were having a spirited argument about where the rugs would appear in the catalog and when they would appear in their shops. Free-for-alls like this never happened in her well-ordered, perfect life back in Atlanta, Alex thought. And all hell broke loose when the subject of pricing was broached. No, Alex was certain this was not the way discussions were held in her family.

"I think Sandy needs time to consider your proposal," he interjected. All talking stopped as the four Grimaldis looked at Sandy.

"By all means," said Joe Grimaldi, as he reached into his pocket for a cigarette.

Caroline smiled. "There are, of course, details to be worked out."

"Plenty of benefit for everyone, though," added Rigo, shifting his gaze from Sandy to Alex, then back to Sandy.

"And as for the risk . . ." began Beth.

"Risk?" Sandy's eyes brightened as she turned toward Alex. "I'm ready for a risk, how about you?" Her open challenge hung in the air between them.

Alex forgot about production costs. He forgot about factory capabilities, shifting personnel, and the price of wool. He forgot about the Grimaldis. In a shimmering pool of light, with the Aegean pounding the shore below them, he saw Sandy. Her soft, daring smile and sure and steady gaze put him off guard. Everything he'd been sure of started to break up, then fought to arrange itself in a new order inside his brain, his heart, his soul. He'd been wrong to think she was some fragile piece of crystal ready to shatter at the least vibration. She welcomed changes, delighted in their possibilities, and grew stronger because of them. He managed a single nod to her question, then asked himself one. Could she accept a change in him?

As the women surrounded Sandy, engaging her in enthusiastic talk, the brothers moved toward Alex, blocking his view of her.

Joe patted him soundly on the back. "How about if we take a tour of this island in the morning, then you and Sandy fly back to Athens with us in the afternoon?"

Rigo raised his glass. "Beth's been missing the kids, and Joe and Caroline figured if you two agreed to pursue this, they'd head back home. Your lawyer can write up a preliminary agreement, and after we sign, we can celebrate tomorrow night."

Alex reached for one of Joe's proffered cigarettes. "If Sandy's agreeable—"

"If Sandy's agreeable?" repeated Joe. "Alex, she's one of the most agreeable people we've met. Isn't that right, Rigo?"

"Right."

The following evening Alex waited his turn in the dimly lit Plaka restaurant for a look through Sandy's photos. They were being passed back and forth among the loudly appreciative Grimaldis. While he waited, he studied the way Sandy's black-velvet bustier molded itself to her breasts. And the way the red-glass disk of one of her earrings brushed her shoulder when she tilted her head to laugh. The flickering candlelight was tinting her face and shoulders the color of warm honey. He massaged his temple as he recalled her tasting like honey and smelling like it too. That her skin would look like warm honey in candlelight was no surprise to him. In the celebratory atmosphere his mood was introspective.

He should have been enjoying the evening more. He'd gotten what he'd wanted. The preliminary contract for the flokatis was signed, and the added bonus of the hand-tufted rugs was in the works.

Joe nudged him. "Sandy's pretty amazing, isn't she?"

"Pretty amazing," Alex agreed, forcing himself not to look at her.

"Yes, sir. She can take these photos back to Atlanta and paint from them there. Or anywhere, for that matter." Joe flipped through the photos. "Aren't they something? Weren't we lucky to find her?"

The dim lights suddenly went out, and a second later a spotlight was directed toward the dance floor. In the hushed moments following, Alex sensed the anticipation building around him. He couldn't have cared less. Snatches of conversation flashed through his brain. "*. . . lucky to find her . . . back to Atlanta . . .*" As strains of a well-known melody began, Alex experienced a paralyzing moment of fear.

Just when he was starting to see Sandy as capable of changing, of making smooth transitions, of accepting at least parts of a world different from her own, he was reminded that she could fly away in a few hours.

Playing faster, the musicians strolled into the room. Several waiters were motioning for the diners to join them in a dance.

"It's that *Zorba the Greek* music. Where's Anthony Quinn when you need him?" Caroline asked, directing a pout toward her husband.

"Right here, darling," said Joe, tapping out the beat on the table. "Care to dance with him?"

As they joined several other people lining up on the dance floor, Beth Grimaldi turned to her husband with an expectant smile on her face.

"I'm not dancing, Beth," insisted Rigo. "We're getting on a plane in three hours, and it's my last chance to talk with Alex."

"Oh, Rigo. That's a contrived excuse, and you know it," said Beth as she turned to Sandy. "I don't know about you, but I'm not leaving Athens before I do this."

"Well, neither am I," said Sandy, bracing her hands on the table and kicking off her black-velvet heels. Without a look in his direction, she scurried onto the dance floor. The black-and-white plaid skirt floated several inviting inches above her knees.

In the last day and a half she'd been as warm and gracious as ever. She'd bantered with him last night, laughed at his jokes during this morning's island tour, and had even politely asked him for his opinion during the business meeting that afternoon. What she hadn't done was look at him the way she used to. The long, deep way that made his heart pound and his blood grow thick with need. And now she was talking about getting in a dance before she left Athens. The knowledge came, stunning him in its simplicity. If he didn't do something about it, she would slip away forever. Alex felt his brow kink as a surge of determination grabbed hold of him, overriding a vague fear that had been plaguing him for weeks. He loosened his tie, pulled it free from his collar, and dropped it onto the seat beside him. As he unbuttoned the top two buttons of his shirt, Rigo turned to look at him.

"Cigarette?" asked Rigo, leaning back in his seat.

"I think I just quit. Thanks anyway," he said, pushing himself out of the booth and up onto his feet. He took off his jacket, then began rolling the sleeves of his shirt up above his elbows. All the time he was watching Sandy, her slender arms stretched across the shoulders of the people on either side of her. A dark cloud of tousled hair floated forward around her face as she concentrated on the intricate footwork. He stepped onto the dance floor and strode over to her. She raised her head as he reached out with one hand and crooked his finger for her to come.

"But I'm just learning how," he heard her say over the music. She was giving him a sunbeam of a smile, which would slay the hardest of hearts; but he knew it was only her second-best smile. He wanted the one that started with a delicate connection to his gut and left him in a haze of heat.

"I'll teach it to you."

She stared into his eyes, and as the delicate connection deepened, her radiant smile softened, washing over him like a warm summer breeze. She lifted her arms, then placed both hands in his. He drew her out onto the center of the floor to the delight and loud applause of everyone around them.

The purpose of the dance was to celebrate the life force within. He knew the steps, had danced them countless times in nightclubs all over the city. But this time, for the first time, he understood the seductive elegance of the dance.

He guided her through her faltering moves, allowing her confidence, like a gentle wave, to grow with each new step. The music was building toward a crescendo, and the crowd clapped out the beat faster and faster. As she twirled beneath his fingertips, her taffeta skirt smacked softly against his thighs. The dance ended with Sandy in his arms, the room on its feet, and his theory of survival in shreds around his heart.

Sandy dropped her head back, then turned in a quarter-circle on her heels. The multitiered chandelier above her in the foyer shimmered with prismed light. "Does this apartment belong to the same Alex Stoner who spits cherry stones across the beach in Zephyros?"

She heard his deep laugh as the door closed behind her with a soft click. "The same."

"One-dimensional, Mr. Stoner, you are not," she teased, looking over her shoulder.

His playful looks continued, as they had since their dance. Without breaking their connected gazes, he tossed his jacket over one of the carved chairs flanking his front door. Except for when they'd danced, he hadn't held her, hadn't really touched her in days.

They were alone, and the sight of his bared arms had her taking a long, slow breath. His shirtsleeves were still rolled above his elbows, and the crisp blond hair sprinkled along his forearms softened the definition of the muscles and cords there. She felt the tension begin to gather in all the right places as he crossed the pink marbled foyer.

"Are you tired?"

"Not a bit."

"Good." As if in invitation, he extended both arms and opened his palms. "There's still time to see the sun rise over the Acropolis."

Disappointment jarred her mood. The clock ticktocked through several voiceless seconds. "Do we have to go out again?"

He chuckled, then wrapped one arm around the top of her shoulders and pulled her against him. "Just onto my balcony."

A minute later they were leaning on the balustrade watching the lights of Athens twinkling on the hills and valley beyond them.

"I feel like we're waiting for the curtain to come up instead of the sun. Which way should I be looking when it happens?"

He stood closer and leaned the side of his face against hers. "Over there, to the right of those two blue lights."

In the cool predawn air the warmth of his face and breath made her want to nuzzle against him. "How much longer?" she asked, trying not to sound breathless from his touch.

He pulled back, then leaned an elbow on the balustrade. "Long enough for us to talk."

He'd hesitated before his reply, giving her a second to look at him. All the good feelings she'd been experiencing concentrated in the pit of her stomach, leaving her weak-kneed and wanting. "About what?"

"Yesterday I explained why I believed we shouldn't make love."

She looked down and ran her thumbnail along the velvet piping connecting the bustier to the taffeta skirt of her dress. She didn't want to hear his serious tone.

"Sandy?"

Don't tell me again, it's for my own good. Don't tell me tonight didn't mean anything to you. She raised her eyes, but instead of meeting his, fixed them on the first orange glimmer above the horizon. "Yes?" *Don't break my heart.*

"Watching you yesterday and today made me realize I don't have the right to decide which risks you should take and which you shouldn't. You're doing a damn fine job of it without unasked-for advice from me."

He shoved his fingers through his hair, then reached for her in one fluid movement. "Sandy, I—" He cupped his hands over her shoulders, stroking the softness there.

The urgency of his touch sent a jolt of pleasure straight to her core.

"I thought I could hold back these feelings, but every time I look at you, I want you more." He ran his fingers down her arms and around to her back, as if memorizing her with each warm caress. "I don't want you to regret . . . Sandy, if you're not ready for this . . ."

Her every nerve ending was quivering with desire for him. Her flesh seemed on fire everywhere he touched her. She lifted her fingers to his lips, stemming his words with her touch and a smile. "I'm ready, Alex."

He pulled back to speak, but gave up the struggle with a groan when she pressed her hips against his. "I'm as ready as you are," she whispered, planting a flurry of kisses against his chin. He dipped lower, catching those kisses, then deepening them as he swirled his tongue over her lips and inside her mouth. His probing sent a molten river of sensation flooding through her body. Instinctively she stepped sideways with him, then twisted in his arms to keep them both standing. When passion threatened to bring her to her knees, he cradled the backs of her thighs and held her closer. With one more hungry kiss, she felt herself swaying, and reached for his shoulders. She stopped fighting gravity when he lifted her up against him and she wrapped both legs around his hips.

Her mouth was wet and ripe for his exploration, and he knew the rest of her was too. He walked them into the bedroom and allowed her to slide her legs down over his hips and thighs.

There was something deliciously clumsy about the way they unbuttoned his shirt and peeled it from his shoulders. Stopping and starting several times, they fell against each other in broken bits of intimate laughter. He kicked off his shoes and was pulling off his socks when she reached to unzip her dress.

"Let me do that."

Barefoot and shirtless, he leaned his forehead against hers and reached behind her. He slid the zipper to the base of her spine, then pulled the dress away from her breasts and began lowering it and himself down the length of her. "You're like a birthday package I've been waiting to unwrap . . . all my life," he murmured, savoring the perfect fit of her soft curves to his hard planes. The dress landed in a whisper of taffeta on the floor around her ankles.

Thrusting her fingers through his hair, she shivered as he pressed his mouth against her, kissing first one breast then the other, then blazing a fiery trail of kisses to her navel. She was wearing beige stockings that hugged the tops of her thighs. Slowly he peeled one down her leg. His careful movements seemed choreographed to drive her mad. He brushed his lips, then his tongue, against the inside of one thigh, as he peeled the next stocking down her leg. Exquisite sensations raced through her, and she clutched his shoulders. Nothing she'd ever experienced had been so richly intense or so blatantly erotic. Holding on to him, she felt the unyielding pleasure deepen as he nuzzled his lips against her. She broke free long enough to hook her thumbs inside the elastic of her lacy white underwear, but it was he who drew them down her legs and steadied her as she stepped out of them and kicked her clothing aside. Desire, like a series of brushfires, flashed between them, threatening to engulf them both.

He stood, unzipped his pants, and pulled off the rest of his clothing.

She reached to take off her earrings.

"Wait."

"Why?" she asked, before she saw the glint of humor in his passion-dark eyes.

"Leave them on." He held his breath until she slowly smiled that gut-grabbing smile.

Cupping her face in his hands, he licked her lips as he lowered her to his bed. Feeling the red-glass disks slide over his fingers, he whispered again, "Just leave them on."

He suckled her breasts till each nipple was pebble hard, and she sighed in ecstasy. He wanted to stroke her, kiss her, touch her for the next hundred years, but the moment his fingers found the liquid heat between her thighs, he felt an overpowering urgency to make his flesh one with hers. She moaned her readiness as his fingers caressed her womanly recesses; then he raised up and let her guide him into her satiny depths. Sinking slowly into her, he held his breath as the white-hot passion threatened to consume him. He felt her quicken around him, then begin to rock against him. When he could trust himself, he began to kiss her again. Slow, hot kisses that deepened with each thrust of his hips.

There wasn't time to think, but she'd done enough of that in the last week anyway. Sensations of rapture continued building within her, heightening her hunger, deepening her desire, driving her closer and closer to a oneness with Alex.

When she cried out his name, he clutched her closer, then joined her in an explosion of molten pleasure.

Afterward he held her in his arms, still stroking her, still kissing her. "Sandy?"

She entwined her fingers in his, complete in his embrace. "Mmmmmm. Yes?"

"We missed the sunrise."

She burrowed deeper into his embrace. "No, we didn't," she whispered.

Eight

From her perch on top of his dresser Sandy sketched Alex, leisurely detailing the musculature of his legs and back. Whether they were tensed with power or deeply relaxed, she knew Alex's muscles intimately. Glancing at the clock on his nightstand, she also knew she had to wake him soon. They had to be at the airport in an hour to greet two wool merchants from New Zealand.

Ever since their return from Athens, Alex had wholeheartedly welcomed her suggestion of entertaining more of his business associates and friends at his Zephyros house. So far she'd managed two beach picnics, one midnight supper, and a rather grand dinner party. And all those wonderful days and nights alone with him in between. By opening up his house and his life, he'd opened up a part of her. He listened to her opinions, asked for her advice, and kept her focused on the present. For the first time in her life someone had handed her the reins and, without restrictions, said, "Go for it!" And she did, in every way. When it came to making love, she was as much thrilled by his spontaneity as by her own. She discovered a voluptuous sensuality she hadn't known she possessed as he made her feel more alive and womanly than she'd ever felt before. Each moment with Alex was complete; it was all she wanted, all she'd ever want.

He turned in his sleep, moving his leg from under the sheet, then shifting it upward on the bed. With parts of him visible from beneath the twisted sheets, he could have been a fallen statue. She surveyed the scene; a sinewy arm and two powerful masculine legs disembodied by a swath of snowy-white percale, his golden head partially hidden under his pillow and one elegant hand curled and hanging over the side of the bed. But though his limbs were reminiscent of Michelangelo's creations, he was no lifeless statue, she reminded herself as she recalled how full of life Alex Stoner had been at one o'clock that morning. Tapping the pencil on her chin, she then drew it slowly across her lips. If thoughts like that continued, she'd never finish the sketch because she'd be crawling in beside him, enflaming him once more as she wrapped herself around his length and covered him with butterfly kisses. Smiling to herself, she thought back over their last few weeks together and knew he'd be only too happy to oblige her.

He turned his head, and she could see that his mouth was still slack with sleep. She lowered the pencil as she continued staring at his mouth. That pagan mouth that had worshiped her body so tantalizingly in the wee hours that morning. She squirmed with pleasure at the memory.

One of his eyes opened. " 'Morning, beautiful."

"Good morning."

"How long have you been there?"

"Not long. You know, you have to be at the airport in an hour to pick up those wool merchants."

"Plenty of time." He bunched the pillow under one ear and rubbed his cheek against it. "Aren't you finished with that yet?"

"My, aren't we grumpy?"

"Well, I'm lonely over here," he mumbled, peeping at her with one eye. He turned his head toward the pillow, but she didn't miss his wily smile.

"Are you really?" Without looking at him, she fingered through her pencil box, pretending that selecting just the right pencil was much more important than his lonely state.

"Yes, really. So, why don't you reach in that top drawer, get out my camera, and take my picture. It's quicker."

"Quicker?" She tossed the pencil back into the box and the sketch pad to the floor before sliding off the dresser. With feigned disappointment, she asked, "Alex, don't you know I do my best work . . . very . . . slowly?"

Both eyes were open now. He propped his chin with one hand and pushed aside the hair falling over his forehead with the other. His eyes lit with interest as they followed her to the bed. "It didn't take you that long last night to—"

She was astride his sheet-draped body in a second. "Hush. You have the naughtiest mouth."

"I thought you liked my mouth. Last night you asked me—"

She clamped her hands over his mouth. "Aren't

you interested in how my sketch of you is coming along? I was having trouble with part of your—"

He pulled her hands away and held them to her sides. "Trouble with one of my parts? And I was sure you'd figured them all out by now." He reached down to lift the sheet. "Perhaps you'd like to study me more closely."

"Honestly, you are incorrigible. It was your ears. They're small ears. Compact and—"

"Maybe I'd better have a look at this sketch," he said, straining his neck to see the pad resting on the flokati beside his bed. "You're not doing one of those Picasso things where I have three eyes, blue hair, and an enormous—"

"Alex!"

Reaching over the edge of the bed, he picked up the pad. "Hmmm . . . just what are these things growing out of my forehead, anyway?"

"What things?" she asked, leaning toward the sketch pad.

"These horns," he said, pointing to some modest tufts of hair. When she leaned closer, he brushed a moist kiss on her neck. The pad slipped back to the floor as he turned to lever one of his legs over her. He reached for the buttons of her cotton eyelet camisole. "You've made me a very passionate guy."

"We're going to be late for the airport," she whispered, as she tugged the sheet away from his hips. Scooting down, she circled his navel with velvety kisses while her fingers worked their artistic magic over the length of him. "Alex?"

"Hmmm?"

"What will you tell them?"

"I'll tell them it was all your fault," he said, closing his eyes with a gasp.

She looked up as Alex emerged from the sea and waved for her to join him. "Hey, birthday girl! Isn't it about time you work up an appetite for your birthday dinner?"

Lifting her brush from the canvas, she looked down at her clothes. Rolled-up shorts and a T-shirt. "I'm right in the middle of painting this sea-scape for you, and besides that, I'm not wearing my swimsuit."

"You're supposed to wear your birthday suit today. It's an old Greek custom."

She tried unsuccessfully to stop a giggle. "I think we've had this conversation before," she said, inching up her hat brim with her paintbrush and tilting her head. If ever she were tempted to forget herself, it was now. She exhaled loudly and closed her eyes, knowing a lifetime of "properness" couldn't be tossed aside easily. "As much as I adore your total lack of inhibition, I"— she looked away—"I just can't picture myself—"

"Bare naked in the great outdoors?" he asked, walking up the beach to where she sat at her easel.

"You're right, even if you are redundant."

"Well, it's worth repeating," he said, leaning over and planting a sensual kiss on her cheek. Lowering himself onto the huge towel beside her, he swiped the water from his face, then rested his chin on his stacked fists. "Anyway, I think I'm wearing down your resistance." He kept his eyes focused at the side of the canvas, waiting for her face to appear there. He smiled when it did.

"Wearing down my resistance? Why do you say that?"

Reaching across the few inches of sand separating them, he ran his fingers over her toes. "The first time you even thought I was skinny-dipping, you didn't know where to look."

She laughed easily. "And now I do?"

"Yes, ma'am, now you do." Settling down to enjoy the sun on his back and Sandy by his side, he closed his eyes and smiled. The days with her were tumbling by in a never-ending parade of pleasures. Running his Athens office from Zephyros had been surprisingly easy. For the first time in his life he knew contentment, and he knew also that Sandy was experiencing it too. Apart from their shared happiness, he had the unique joy of watching her test her capabilities as an artist and businesswoman, and come up a winner on both counts. He was aware that the patterns of his life were changing as he wove Sandy's presence into them day by day. The only unsettling element was a vague sense of apprehension when she was out of his sight.

"I think Harry and George enjoyed their trip out here, don't you?" she asked.

Alex pictured the two New Zealanders on rented motor bikes zipping around the island last week. The exuberant twosome appeared to enjoy Zephyros except for one thing. " 'All this place needs is a tennis court, mate,' " Alex said in a respectable rendition of a New Zealand accent as he looked at Sandy. "What's with the raised eyebrows? I thought I had that accent down pat."

Sandy shrugged. "I have to admit, I've missed playing tennis myself."

He studied the faraway look in her eyes and felt apprehension spread through his chest. "Did you play a lot back in Atlanta?"

"Oh, yes. I used to play three, sometimes four, times a week at the club." She nibbled her bottom lip as her mind seemed to drift to other things.

His biggest doubt used to be that she would never feel comfortable with his lifestyle. That she'd not only embraced it, but managed to change it for the better had made him happier than he'd ever been. Now, with this damned tennis thing to remind her of Atlanta, he had to wonder if she was tiring of this endless holiday. He raised up on his elbows. "Sandy?"

"Yes?"

He scooped up a handful of sand, then let it trickle into a conical pile in front of his towel. Why did he feel like a scared kid? "You're writing more letters lately, and you receive them almost every day too. I have a feeling you're beginning to miss your friends and family more than you're telling."

She lifted the brush from her canvas, quirked her lips, and nodded. "They can drive me up a wall sometimes with all their attention and concern, but, yes, I do miss them." She scratched the end of her nose. "What about you? Living halfway around the world like this, don't you ever miss your family? You know, you never talk about them."

He stood up and pulled on his shorts.

"Alex? Did I say something wrong?"

He shook his head. "I never talk about them because mine wasn't a happy family like yours."

"I thought it might be something like that. But I'd like to hear about them anyway, because they're yours." Her soft southern drawl coaxed him.

He studied her for a moment, then leaned a shoulder against a rock wall. "When we were up at Delphi, right before you fell, you said you'd had a perfect life. Well, I didn't have a perfect life, Sandy. My mother left me and my father for another man. I was five at the time, and all my father told me was that she didn't want us anymore and we were never going to see her again. I grew up thinking it was somehow my fault."

A poignant expression settled on her face. "Oh, Alex, I'm sorry. I've read that children always think they're to blame for a parent's desertion. . . ."

He shrugged. "Anyway, we hit the road the day he told me. We kept on moving. Never stayed in one place for very long." His laugh was short and harsh. "Dad and I were not Norman Rockwell material. We celebrated Thanksgiving with turkey TV dinners. The most time I ever spent in one place was at Braxton University."

She stood up and walked toward him. "Go on," she said softly. "I want to hear it all."

He pulled her into his arms, and she kissed his forehead. "About a year after my father died, my mother found me and told me she'd been trying all along to track me down. She said things hadn't been right between them for a long time, and when he found out she'd been seeing someone, he swore to her she'd never see me again."

Sandy reached up and ran her fingers through his hair. "You sound like you still don't quite believe her."

"I don't know if I do or not. My dad was the one person who was always there for me. I was his whole life." He took Sandy's hand and kissed it. "When my mother and I finally got together, she seemed happy to see me, but I . . . I couldn't quite connect with her."

Sandy stepped out of his arms to face him squarely. "It's hard to let go of the past, to move on."

Shifting his gaze toward the water, he blew out a puff of air from between pursed lips.

"You know you have to do it, Alex. And I have faith in you—I know you will."

He shook his head and snorted. "Tea and sympathy, is it?" He pushed away from the rock and headed for the steps. "This can't be wiped away with a greeting card."

She went after him, stilling him when she grabbed his arm. "There are always two sides to every story. I can't speak for your father or your mother, but I can surely speak from my own experience."

"Your own experience?"

"I don't want to shatter any more illusions about Jackson, but I'm going to tell you some things about him because it just might help you put things in perspective. You knew him once as a friend. I knew him as a wife, and my family knew him as 'Sandy's perfect husband.' In his own way he loved me, but he was demanding and inflexible, dedicated to making me into his version of the perfect wife."

"What do you mean?"

"Even though he knew how much my painting meant to me, he thought it took too much time away from being Mrs. Jackson Benedict. Maybe he was even jealous. Anyway, he decided I'd be a better wife if I gave up painting altogether and dedicated all my time to him. And he succeeded, because I was young when we married and utterly vulnerable to his criticism. Then there were my friends, few of whom met with his approval. He made them so uncomfortable with his superior airs that they stopped coming around. Sometimes I thought I'd go crazy in that big house of his and that narrow little world he'd created. Alex, he even reached out from the grave to 'guide' his widowed wife."

"From the grave? I don't understand."

"People can do such awful things in the name of love. He'd decided, that after a respectful period of mourning I should remarry."

Alex nodded. "Go on."

"He took it upon himself to choose the lucky man, and then, shortly before he died, he told my parents. About six months ago they introduced his choice to me." She shook her head and laughed. "He was so much like Jackson. What really mattered to me was that my parents finally came to their senses and told me about it."

"Jackson actually chose someone to be your next husband?"

She pointed her finger at him. "Yes. Like your father keeping you and your mother separated all those years, Jackson did what he thought was best for me. Only he never asked me what I thought or wanted, just like your father never asked you."

"That was different. I was a child, Sandy."

"But you grew up."

Alex lowered his head for a moment, then looked out to sea. "I don't know, Sandy, I just don't know. So much time has passed. She has another husband and children. And grandchildren."

She took his chin on her fingertips and made him look at her. "Life is too short, Alex. Let her love you. Let yourself love her."

" 'Let her love you. Let yourself love her,' " he repeated, smiling tenderly at her. "That easy, huh?"

"It can be." Returning to her art supplies, she began tightening the caps on the tubes of paint in the box.

"Sandy, don't be angry. I didn't mean to sound ungrateful for your confidences."

"You haven't made me angry. I just got to thinking about my mom and dad and how much I miss them. I want to go up to the house and see if I can get a call through before we meet Bertram and Claire for dinner. Would you bring the easel and the rest of this when you come?"

His heart was beating just a little too fast. "Why call them now?"

"Just to know if Daddy's holding his golf score below eighty and if mother's received that ring I sent her." She winked at him before lifting the painting between her fingers and hurrying up the steps with it. "You know, I think you'd like my folks."

He could feel it starting to happen. First the phone call. Then the announcement he'd been dreading all along would come. She was beginning her first steps back to her life in Atlanta.

• • •

"How about a coffee before we head back?" Alex asked as they walked under a string of lights crisscrossing the waterfront promenade.

"I'd love a cup," she said, sitting down at an empty table bordering the promenade.

"Are you going to try again to get that call through to your parents?"

"Yes, I thought I would," she answered, turning her face to the open water beyond the harbor. "Oh, Alex, look. I can see the ferry coming in. It's so mysterious, lit up like that out there in the dark."

Alex took her hand and squeezed it as a waiter approached them. After he ordered, he leaned back, drew in a long breath, and stared at the salt and pepper shakers. His contemplative mood intrigued her. Ever since they'd left Bertram's, he'd been quiet. "Thank you for that intimate little birthday dinner with Bertram and Claire."

Drumming his fingers on the white tablecloth, he gave her a quick smile. "Hmmm? Oh, you're welcome."

She leaned forward giving his arm a slight shake. "Alex, did you hear what I just said?"

He blinked. "I'm sorry, what?"

"I thanked you for that intimate little birthday dinner that turned out to be a surprise party with eighteen of the craziest people I've ever known. Bertram said you'd been planning it for two weeks." She leaned in close to his face and crossed her eyes. "Do you remember any of these details?"

He gave her a closed-mouth smile. "Yes, of course I do. I was just . . . thinking about some things." He worked his jaw muscles, tensing them, then relaxing them again and again.

"What's wrong? You look one pout short of miserable."

He pulled back as their coffee was placed before them. "Costa, bring me a pack of cigarettes and put it on the bill." Reaching for two packets of sugar, he slapped them softly against his palm before tearing them open. " 'One pout short of miserable'?" he repeated.

"Yes." She watched him pour in the sugar, then stir the rich, dark liquid. "And for the life of me, I can't understand why. It was such a wonderful party, and except for you wrestling Bertram to the ground when he insisted you wear one of his kilts, I thought you were enjoying yourself."

"I was."

He looked up at her, studying every detail of her face. The intensity of his gaze never lightened as he brushed back her hair and stroked her cheek. "You look so sexy in that," he said, staring at the short navy-blue silk sarong-style dress, that hugged her willowy body so well. "You're the most beautiful woman here."

"Well, that seems only fair, since I'm sitting next to the most handsome man." She expected a comic reaction but didn't get one. Again, he gave her a closed-mouth, almost sad smile, then returned his attention to his coffee. He wanted to talk, she was certain of that, but he'd managed to veer away once again.

She looked toward the ferry boat as the passengers began disembarking onto the pier. The scene was magical and mysterious, but it didn't stop her from thinking about Alex's strange mood. He'd gone out of his way to make her party a riot of fun. Why, she wondered, was he so uncomfortable with her now? She turned to him, determined to find out what was wrong.

"Alex, if there's someth—"

He drew a long blue-velvet case from his blazer pocket and placed it before her on the table. "I wanted to give you this when we were alone. Go ahead. Open it."

She steadied the thin case with one hand as she lifted the lid with her thumb. "Oh, Alex." She shut the case with a snap. "My Lord, they're the most beautiful things I've ever seen."

Laughing for the first time in half an hour, he took the case from her hands and opened it a second time. "You're not supposed to keep these shut up," he said, removing the necklace. "You're supposed to wear them." He held up the strand of pure white perfectly matched pearls with the M&M-size ruby centerpiece. "Try on the earrings while I figure out this clasp."

"Pearls and rubies. I adore them together," she whispered, picking up the earrings.

"That's what you said the day you picked out the ring for your mother."

"How ever did you remember that?" she asked removing diamond studs from her earlobes and replacing them with the clusters of pearls and rubies.

He looked at her long and hard as he fought back a smile. "Ever since you mentioned how much you liked them, I've pictured you several times in pearls and rubies. Believe me, those images are unforgettable." He fastened the necklace around her neck, then sat back to look at her. So did several ferry passengers as they found their way from the boat to the cozy waterside restaurant.

"Well, do I do justice to those images?" she asked with a teasing smile.

"Yes and no," he replied, infusing the answer with a comical uncertainty. "Sandy, you are some kind of wonderful," he whispered leaning forward to kiss her. His hands rested on her thighs.

"So are you," she said, kissing him back. Thank heaven he was sounding like his old self again. She placed her hands on his shoulders and her forehead on his as she sighed. "Thank you for my beautiful birthday presents. You always make me feel so good." That serious look was clouding his eyes again. "Hey," she continued in the same joyful vein, "What is it? What's got you down?"

"This whole summer's been very special for you, hasn't it?"

As more people arrived at the restaurant, she leaned forward for privacy. "You know it has. You've opened up the world for me."

"It's been . . . very special for me, too, Sandy."

She fingered the pearls at her throat. He'd cherished her as no other man ever could. She'd given her best to him. And in return he'd introduced her to so many new joys. She ached for him to open up and tell her what was in his heart. She watched as he rubbed his mouth and moved uncomfortably in his chair. *Ask me to stay.*

"So when are your art classes scheduled to start?"

"My art classes? The fourteenth of September." An anxious silence ballooned between them. "I'm going to have to make some calls about that." Touching an earring, she pushed back the idea that the jewelry could be his good-bye gift to her.

"And what about Atlanta, Sandy?"

"Atlanta?" She licked her lip. "What about Atlanta?"

"You tried calling your parents three times before the party. You said your best friend wrote you and wants you in her wedding. The social season's about to pick up back there." He turned the cigarette pack over and over on the table. "Just how much have you been missing that life?"

The light bulb suddenly went on inside her head. Of course he wanted her to stay. He'd simply never been in the position of having to ask. And knowing how he'd been hurt in his childhood, she was certain he didn't want to chance any sort of rejection again. He'd been careful through the years when it came to commitments. She'd heard bits and pieces about his past through his friends. Women had tried to move in on him numerous times, but Alex had insisted on living alone.

"Alex, I'm never going to live my old life again. How could you think that after all that's happened this summer?"

His expression softened into an endearing mix of hope and confusion.

Laughing quietly, she brushed a tear from her

cheek and shook her head. "Now, is there something else you want to ask me?"

Just as he felt capable of forming a coherent sentence, a voice with a cultured southern accent called from the promenade, "Sandy? Is that you, darling?" Then another, deeper voice called out, "Sandra Elizabeth Patterson, get over here and give your daddy a hug!"

"Oh, my goodness, Alex. I can't believe this." Her hands flew to her face, but not before he saw the look of delight there.

Nine

As Sandy welcomed her parents with tears and laughter, Alex experienced a myriad of conflicting emotions. Seeing her surprised and happy warmed his heart. So had her smile and tears moments before when she insisted that she wasn't going to live that old life again. But as he watched her being enveloped in the arms of her adoring parents, he felt himself descending to a level of loneliness he'd never want to experience again. And then there was that quick, sharp stab of jealousy. He could never remember his parents sharing such a full, loving moment with him like this.

That old feeling of not belonging crawled up into his heart. He felt like an outsider, an intruder, for witnessing the intimate exchanges taking place before him. Just when he thought he might slip away into the darkness, Sandy's laughter reminded him of warmth and light. She was trying to rub a smear of lipstick from her father's face as her mother attempted the same with her.

As Sandy's father swiped at his cheek with his handkerchief, Alex tossed a few coins on the table and started for the threesome. As he stepped around three suitcases and a bag of golf clubs, he took his own handkerchief from his pocket and put it in Sandy's outstretched hand.

After dabbing at her cheek, Sandy pressed her hand to her chest to still her laughter. Forcing a steadying breath into her lungs, she looked at Alex. "Daddy, Mother, this is Alex Stoner."

Her mother took his hand in both of hers. Her brown eyes twinkled with genuine affection. "I feel like I already know you, Alex. Sandy's told us so much about you in her letters. It's such a pleasure to meet you at last."

The slim, silver-haired woman exuded a heartfelt warmth that had him cursing himself for his initial jealousy. "It's a pleasure to meet you too, Mrs. Patterson," he said, accepting a kiss on his cheek.

Déjà vu struck with a fist as he inhaled Mrs. Patterson's Chantilly. His own mother had always worn Chantilly. Struggling to regain his composure, he offered his hand to Sandy's father. "Mr. Patterson."

As Sandy's father disengaged an arm from his daughter's embrace, Alex didn't miss the quick sizing-up Sandy's father gave him.

"Call me R.J." His handshake was a firm, no-nonsense grip, even though his other arm remained around Sandy's waist. "Can't thank you enough for taking care of Sandy after she hurt her wrist."

Alex managed a smile as Mrs. Patterson reached for her daughter's hand.

"Oh, sugar, how is that wrist? We were so worried about you."

"Your mother canceled our golfing vacation in Arizona to come over here and kiss your boo-boo all better. Eight days at a PGA course!" R.J. raised his hand in an effort to fend off a mock blow from his wife.

The good-natured razzing continued around Alex. "R.J., stop telling her those lies. Actually it was your father who insisted we come." Mrs. Patterson turned to Alex. "Do tell him there's a golf course at the Hotel Apollo. That's where we've made reservations."

Alex raised his eyebrows. "There's not a golf course anywhere on this island."

"A putting green?" asked R.J. in an effort to connect with Alex. "Tell me there's a putting green, Alex."

Alex shook his head.

"Sandy, how have you lived in such a primitive place all these weeks and come out looking so happy?" her father asked with pretended severity. Before Sandy could answer, her father turned to her mother. "You were right, Olivia. We've got to get this girl back where she belongs. Back to Live Oaks Country Club."

As comical as R.J. Patterson meant to sound, Alex sensed there was more than a modicum of seriousness to his words.

Sandy looked at her parents and then at Alex. She didn't bother hiding her smile. "Y'all would be surprised how well I've managed in this primitive place."

Alex's flagging spirits suddenly picked up as her gaze locked with his. Hoping the moment would hold, he nodded to the Pattersons. "There's plenty of room at my house, and since there's no golfing at the Apollo, there's no reason to stay all the way over there."

"Oh, we couldn't possibly intrude," said Mrs. Patterson.

R.J. slipped his hand into his pocket. Although he continued smiling, his voice took on a more serious tone. "She's right, Alex. We were thinking about surprising Sandy, not about barging in on you."

"You won't be," he said, picking up a suitcase.

"Are you certain?" asked Olivia Patterson. "We don't mean to disrupt your plans."

"No problem, Mrs. Patterson. We're quite flexible about schedules out here. Right, Sandy?"

"Right."

Alex watched her gaze swing like a pendulum between him and her parents. The Pattersons couldn't have picked a worse day, a worse hour, a worse moment, to come. He'd traveled through a mine field of emotions to get to where he was with Sandy just minutes ago. When he'd finally allowed himself to believe that anything was possible because she'd put her past life behind her, two tempting reminders from that life had appeared. That they happened to be such nice people wasn't helping.

"Look up and smile. That's my girls," her father said. "Now let's try one putting your arms around each other."

"R.J., this is the very last photo," Mrs. Patterson

insisted as she put her arm around her smiling daughter.

"Nonsense, Olivia. After this I want a shot of you two inside by those frescoes."

They were spending one of their last vacation days touring the island's fifteenth-century monastery. The week had been an especially pleasant one, filled with plenty of touring and shopping interspersed with catch-up conversation and, thankfully, nonintrusive references to her relationship with Alex. Sandy's only complaint, a silent one, was that Alex hadn't joined in the activities. He'd spent most of the days at the house working on his export business.

Mrs. Patterson patted her daughter's hand, then bowed her head and adjusted the peridot ring on her own hand. Her nervous fiddling soon had Sandy's riveted attention. "Mother, is there something you're not telling me? Is someone sick back home? Is it Grandfather?"

"No, dear. It's just that I want to ask you something and I don't know how to."

Sandy sat up straighter and put her arm around her mother's shoulder. "You can ask me anything," she said, feeling more like a parent than a child for the first time in her life. The strange feeling needed getting used to.

"It's taken this trip to Greece for your father and me to finally see what you were trying to tell us for so long." Her mother looked toward R.J. as she wrapped her hands around her knees and sighed. "Maybe we have been smothering you with too much attention these past few years. I guess we picked up where Jackson left off. We even tried to marry you off again to that Charles Taylor Richardson, like Jackson asked us to."

"Mother, I haven't thought about that for ages. You didn't think I was still upset, did you?"

"Well, isn't that the reason you came to Greece?"

"No. That's not the reason." She stood up and leaned against the curved wall of the stairway. *Well, only part of it,* she thought charitably. "I wanted to travel. I wanted to paint. I needed to be on my own for once."

"I told your mother she was dramatizing," her father said as he approached them. "I told her, 'Our Sandy doesn't know how to hold a grudge.'" R.J. beamed. "It warms my heart to see you painting again, honey. This business arrangement with the Grimaldis and your sales at Bertram MacDougall's gallery have made us proud."

"Thank you, Daddy."

Her mother slipped her hanky inside the sleeve of her sweater. "But you've stayed in Greece much longer than we expected." She licked her lips nervously. "Darling, it—it isn't just your art sales keeping you here, is it?"

Her parents were leaving tomorrow. It would be unfair to see them off without some sort of explanation. But what could she tell them? She stared at the toes of her red tennis shoes as she smoothed her hands over her jeaned thighs. How in heaven's name was she going to explain that although Alex hadn't asked her to stay and he hadn't even said he loved her, she knew he was going to the next moment they were alone. She squeezed her eyes closed.

"Sandy?"

She couldn't give Olivia and R.J. Patterson details, but she could give them reassurance with her straightforward honesty. "It's Alex."

A pregnant silence blossomed inside the walls of the monastery as her parents exchanged a long, slow look. This was it, Sandy thought. The true test as to whether or not they saw her as a new, independent person, capable of making her own decisions.

Her father spoke first. "I won't embarrass you by asking Alex if his intentions are honorable. I just want you to know, I've never seen you look happier."

"Thank you, Daddy," she said, slipping into his bear-hug embrace. A surge of affection washed over her. "This means so much to me," she whispered. *One down, one to go,* she thought, peeking at her mother.

With less enthusiasm than her husband, Mrs. Patterson joined them in the embrace. She rested her cheek on her daughter's shoulder. "We are proud of you. We just miss you so darn much. When are you coming home?" After a few seconds of silence Mrs. Patterson raised her head. "Sandy?"

"I don't know."

"You haven't mentioned anything about marriage. What about art school? That'll be starting—"

"I'm reconsidering the need for art school."

"Olivia." Sandy's father stared into his wife's eyes. "We just told her how proud we are of her. We just told her we've never seen her look happier. We'll trust her to make the right decision about this matter."

"Surely by Christmas," her mother remarked, wide-eyed.

Mr. Patterson dipped his head to sharpen the eye contact with his wife. "We'll trust her, Olivia. Won't we?"

Mrs. Patterson bit her lip. "Yes."

"And we won't insist she share with us any more than she wants to right now."

Mrs. Patterson nodded.

He gave his daughter a tender look. "You've done a lot of changing this summer, Sandy. It becomes you."

The next afternoon Sandy stood over the kitchen table cutting out rows of star-shaped cookies with her mother. As the smell of brandy, almonds, and rose water wafted through the air, she could hear her dad putting golf balls across the living-room floor. As usual, Alex was in his office.

"What did you say they were called again?" asked Olivia as she carefully placed the unbaked cookies on a baking sheet.

"*Kourabiethes.*" Her mother's nervous chatter hadn't let up once today. "Are you certain this is how you wanted to spend your last day in Greece? We could have taken a picnic lunch to the olive grove I told you about. Or down to the beach."

"*Kourabiethes.* There, I knew I could say that. No, no. This is exactly what I wanted to do."

Sandy set the cookie cutter aside and wiped her hands on her apron. "What is it?" she asked softly. "What's wrong?"

Mrs. Patterson hesitated as she lifted another star-shaped cookie onto the baking sheet. "Nothing."

"Yes, there is," she said. She saw the strained cheerfulness disappear from her mother's face.

"I—I know your father doesn't want me dwelling on this, but I've missed you. I miss our shopping trips and baking bread on Wednesdays and our Friday dinners at the club." Olivia stared out the open window at the perfectly blue Aegean. "Are you upset with me because I feel that way?" She lifted the filled cookie sheet from the table, then paused to look out the window.

"No. I'd be surprised if you didn't miss those things a little."

"I do," said her mother with tears streaming down her face.

Sandy swallowed the lump in her throat and nodded. "You know, I couldn't have stayed Jackson's noble widow or your little girl forever. I had to go out and make my own life. Create a new me. You have to learn to accept those things so that we can both go on with our lives." Sandy laughed quietly. "So Daddy can take you out to Arizona."

For a long while Olivia Patterson continued to stare at the Aegean as tears ran down her face. Then, setting the cookie sheet back down on the table, she wiped her eyes and smiled at her daughter. "If I can learn to call brandied shortbread *kourabiethes*, I can learn to accept the new you."

Embracing her mother, Sandy whispered, "I knew you could."

"But I hope you'll be home for Christmas, Sandy.

It's such a special time for all of us. You could bring Alex. . . ."

She gave her mother one more squeeze. Why not put her fears to rest? Sandy thought. "Christmas," she said, picturing Alex next to her by the Christmas tree . . . sipping nutmeg-sprinkled eggnog from a silver cup . . . herself proudly introducing him to every relative within a five-hundred-mile radius of Atlanta . . . wedding him on Christmas Eve. She hugged her mother closer. "I wouldn't miss this Christmas in Atlanta for anything."

"What are you two going to do with all these cookies?" asked Mr. Patterson as he entered the kitchen.

Sniffing back the tears, both women pulled away and looked at each other.

"I have no idea," said Sandy before bursting into laughter.

Through several fits of laughter Olivia said, "If they don't arrest me for smuggling, I guess I could take them back to the Christmas bazaar committee. What do you think, Sandy?"

Before she could answer, a theatrical cough sounded through the kitchen. All three Pattersons turned toward the second doorway leading to the hall.

"And not leave any for me, Mrs. Patterson?"

"There you are." Sandy brushed her apron, then walked into Alex's arms.

She was as bubbly as a glass of champagne. He kissed her lightly on the lips, then looked into her face. Looking for something he could recognize.

Some sign that they would pick up where they'd left off once her parents left. Was he staring too hard?

"We've had such a wonderful week together," she told him as she swung around to her parents.

"We can't thank you enough for having us, Alex," Olivia said. "We've all had such a lovely time."

"Amen," R.J. concurred.

"The best time," Sandy agreed, holding onto Alex's hand. She turned to him. "The very best time, Alex."

He didn't doubt it for a second. Not with her sparkling smile, her tendency to keep squeezing his hand, and the powdered sugar on her nose and arms. He allowed her to draw him out of the kitchen and into the living room.

"Alex Stoner," she said in a warning voice as she tugged at his buttons. "You've been ignoring us all week."

What could he tell her? That he'd heard their laughter ringing through the house and he'd reached for his door handle fifty times, then pulled his hand away fifty more? That he'd cursed himself for a fool for getting so involved with her? That he'd thought his heart was turning to stainless steel because of the emptiness echoing there for the past six days?

"You didn't need me intruding on your family reunion. It looks as though you had a pretty nice time."

She let go of his buttons and wrapped her arms around his waist. "Alex, it's been great. They've changed. They've really changed."

"Have they?" Staring blankly at the white stucco

wall in front of him, he felt the loneliness approaching. There was nothing he could do to stop it.

"Yes, because they've finally accepted that I'm not their little girl anymore. Everything is so relaxed between us now. Daddy's been just plain marvelous. And Mother's already involving me in her Christmas activities."

Christmas. "I wouldn't miss this Christmas in Atlanta for anything." He couldn't put those words out of his mind. They were the first ones he'd heard as he'd reached the kitchen door. Dammit, why hadn't he broken this off weeks ago? He reached into his pocket and drew out his cigarettes. After lighting one, he looked at her with a closed-mouth smile. "I knew things would eventually work out."

Her eyes narrowed to skeptical slits. "Did everything go okay with that last phone call?"

"Sure. Why do you ask?"

"I don't know," she said, shrugging uneasily. "You seem a little tense."

He plowed his fingers through his hair. "Sorry. I do have a lot on my mind. I haven't been around the Athens office much this summer."

"I see," she said, turning away and walking to the fireplace. She ran her hand over the blue and green tiles beneath the mantel.

What the hell was the matter with him? She was already slipping away—did he have to push her too? Stubbing out his cigarette, he went to her, cloaking her in his embrace. "When do I get you alone?"

Immediately he felt her relax and burrow back into his arms. "Tonight."

He was sick at heart when he remembered that

she would be leaving soon too. Inhaling her fragrance, he pressed a kiss to her temple and wondered what waking up would be like without his body curled around hers. How many more nights would he hold this heaven in his arms? He should ask her, then get on with enjoying what time they had left. *Just ask her, dammit!* What had Jackson said to Sandy all those years ago about him? "Alex Stoner's not afraid. . . ." Wrong, old buddy.

With her parents gone, there were no social distractions to disguise it any longer. Something about Alex *was* different. He wasn't interested in her attempt to resume their usual teasing banter either. He kissed her several times, but no knowing smile drifted onto his face afterward. No evidence remained of the playful, naughty boy in Alex. What had happened? Where was the joy? When would it return?

While she pondered those questions, one thing she knew hadn't changed. The need between them was stronger than ever. She read it in his eyes, saw it in the way his pagan lips parted each time he looked at her, knew it by the slight flare of his nostrils each time she looked back. His desire was almost tangible. And it matched her own.

Her curiosity, like her arousal, was in full flower by the time they were alone. He was a few feet away from her, removing his cuff links, unbuttoning his shirt . . . staring at her from some different place in his soul. A deep, needy, wordless place she hadn't been aware of before tonight. Feminine instinct urged her to reach out and explore it. Knowing how he loved to watch her take off her clothes, she peeled them away with slow and exquisite care. With her shoes and clothes in a pile next to her, she reached for the catch on her necklace. He shook his head. Then she remembered something he'd said the night he'd given it to her. Stepping closer, she trailed her fingers over the necklace.

"Is this the way you were imagining I'd look in rubies and pearls?" she asked seductively.

Taking her hand away, he held it in the space between them. The window light from the patio accentuated the intensity of his gaze as he drank her in.

"Almost," he said, raising her hand to his mouth, then pressing her thumb to his lips.

He sucked it slowly into his mouth. As he swirled his tongue around it, the only sound was her sharp intake of air. She was breathing rapidly through her mouth by the time he performed the erotic act on two more of her fingers. When he'd finished, her eyes were closed, and every nerve ending on her body was begging for similar attention. She was past the point of polite inquiries. "Tell me what you want, Alex." *Tell me what you need.* He lowered her hand and pressed it against him.

"Pleasure," he said, taking her down on the white flokati. Sliding his hand over her breast, he gently tugged at her nipple, bringing it to a tumescent peak, then moved his hand to the honeyed warmth between her thighs.

She knew what he wanted, and she gave it to him. Caressing . . . stroking . . . wet, hot kisses . . . skin against skin . . . whispered pleas . . . the holding back . . . then caresses gone mad . . . and that final frenzied struggle of giving and receiving . . . and being.

When he tried to ease himself out of her, she held him in. "Alex, I'll always love you."

He looked away and swallowed. He thought he could survive her departure, but he was now a dying man. She'd delivered his sentence with a satin-wrapped bullet, the mother of all exit lines. *"I'll always love you."* He drew away, but she didn't let go.

"Alex? Alex, say something. Talk to me."

He'd wanted the never-ending fantasy back. "More, Sandy," he said, entering her again. His voice was a ragged whisper now. "I want more."

And she gave him more.

Ten

The space next to her in bed was empty, but she knew where Alex was before she opened her eyes. She pictured him doing what he loved to do in the morning, swimming naked in the sea. She smiled slowly. There was a magical quality about that beach and the refreshing saltwater of the Aegean. Each time they'd been together down there, Alex had revealed something new about himself. Perhaps this morning he'd finish that conversation he'd started last week. And joining him in a swim was a fabulous way to say good morning to the man she loved.

After putting on her swimsuit and shrugging into his robe, she headed out of the room and through the house. As another smile began lighting her face, she stepped out onto the patio—and stopped dead in her tracks. He was standing at the far end of the patio with his hands braced against the rail. And he was wearing a business suit.

"Alex?"

He looked over his shoulder, then looked back at the sea for a few seconds before turning around to face her. "Good morning."

"Good morning." His tie was knotted, the collar

of his pale-blue shirt was crisp with starch, and his black shoes were polished to perfection. "Why are you dressed like that?" she asked, motioning to his clothing. When he didn't answer right away, she walked barefoot across the patio, hesitating a few feet from him.

A renegade breeze tugged at his tie, but he tucked it back into his jacket. "I have to catch the ten A.M. flight to Athens."

"You didn't mention it yesterday." She twisted the white terry sash in her hands as fear began needling her stomach.

"You know me. I hate to kill a good time," he said lightly, as he reached into his jacket for a cigarette. He could get through this, he reminded himself. Quick, clean, over and out. He'd played this scene numerous times before, as a child and as an adult.

She nodded in slow motion. "I see. When will you be back?"

He cupped his hand around the cigarette, struck a match, and when he finally exhaled, looked up at her. "That's the thing. Not for quite a while. You see, I've put off those factory-inspection tours too long. Then I've got banking business in Zurich, and after that some friends have invited me to Corfu. You'll be back in the States and starting art school before I see this place again."

Even as she felt the rug being pulled out from under her, her proper upbringing, like a reflex, kicked in. She pressed both hands to her chest. "Well, this is quite a surprise," she managed before forcing a trembling smile onto her face.

"I don't know how to thank you for . . . everything."

He examined the end of his cigarette. "You don't have to. It was a pleasure having your company, Sandy." He rubbed the back of his neck. "Look, I hate long good-byes. You can stay on as long as you like, just let Bertram know when you're leaving. And I'll have my office contact you later today about the Grimaldi business." He checked his watch. "My taxi's probably pulling up about now." He put his arm around her shoulder. "Walk me to the door, okay?"

She took a deep breath. "Sure," she said, struggling to remember why she had to be brave and gracious while he ate her heart for breakfast.

"I haven't seen you all summer, my friend," said Dimitri as he placed another cup of coffee in front of Alex. "Rumor has it you were kidnapped by a goddess, held hostage in your own house, and tortured for your love secrets."

As miserable as Alex felt, he gave in to halfhearted laughter. "You can't believe everything you hear," he said, reaching for another cigarette. When he realized he had one lit in the ashtray, he offered the second to the woman next to him. A couple of days away from Sandy and he couldn't count to two. He rubbed his temple. Self-doubt had plagued him since the plane lifted off from Zephyros yesterday morning. He felt like knocking a hole in the wall. What the hell was he doing here?

"And you smoke too many cigarettes." Dimitri

stared at Alex for a minute, then sat down beside him. "Perhaps you'd be better off satisfying that sweet tooth."

Before Alex could reply, the short, curly-haired woman next to him made a disgusted sound with her tongue. "Alex does not like sweets, Dimitri," she said in heavily accented English. "He likes more exotic treats. Don't you, Alex?" Placing her hand on his knee, she repeated the question. When he didn't answer, she reached for his coffee, drinking neatly from his cup. "Anyway, he will not tell me where he has been all summer. It is some large secret that makes him miserable, Dimitri. What shall I do to make him forget his misery?"

Alex crossed his arms and leaned forward to plant his elbows on the table. Whatever had prompted him to call Tina was lost under one screaming thought— inviting her to spend the day with him had been a stupid mistake. The two men looked at each other, then Dimitri got up and shrugged.

"Tina, I don't think there is anything you can do for Alex."

"Of course there is," she said, sliding her hand up Alex's thigh under cover of the table. "Nothing has changed for Alex and me."

A very stupid mistake. But he realized why he'd called Tina. He knew he could be into mindless activity with her in a matter of minutes, and then he wouldn't have to think about Sandy. There was a sick, impractical joke somewhere in that plan, but it had taken until this moment to see who the victim of the joke was. Him.

There was no force on earth capable of taking his

mind off Sandy. Certainly not the hollow pleasure of the woman hanging over him. "Actually Tina," he said, removing her hand, "there have been changes."

"Really?" She backed off, inhaled deeply from her cigarette, then blew a vertical stream of smoke into the air above their heads. "And will these changes prevent you from going to Corfu with me next week, Alex?"

Alex looked from Tina to Dimitri and back to Tina. Bertram had called him that morning to tell him Sandy was leaving in the afternoon, and if he didn't come to his senses, he might very well never see her again. When Alex had tried arguing that Sandy had already decided to go back to her old life, Bertram had called him a fool and hung up. Bertram was right. He was a fool. He'd been a fool when he let Sandy believe that memories of Jackson kept them apart. A fool when he'd told himself he was saving Sandy pain and confusion by not getting close to her. And a complete idiot if he didn't catch her before she walked out of his life and back to her old one.

"Alex, you haven't answered me." Tina smoothed her short white leather skirt over her legs.

"Sorry, Tina. I'm not going to make it to Corfu," he said, stubbing out his cigarette. He checked his watch and winced. "Dimitri, I need to use your phone. It's an emergency."

Before Dimitri could speak, Tina interrupted. "What did you mean, you can't make it to Corfu?"

Alex reached into his pocket. "How much, Dimitri?"

Dimitri smiled as he waved away Alex's request for

the bill. "Today you were my guest, and the phone is in the kitchen."

Tina's eyes narrowed with simmering anger. "What is this emergency? I demand to know."

"His mother," said Dimitri.

Alex patted the *taverna* owner on the shoulder as he headed inside. "Her too."

Sooner or later the pain of her heartache was going to hit full force, and she wanted to be off the island before that happened. Sandy loaded the last of her luggage into the trunk of Alex's car and went back for her paints. Looking around the living room one last time, her gaze came to rest on the seascape she'd painted for him. They'd never gotten around to framing it, and it still stood unadorned on the easel. She kept staring at the seductive scene; the beige crescent beach, the sunlight glinting off the water, and the red-and-orange-striped beach umbrella with the flapping fringe. Not that it would change the nature of one grain of sand on that beach, one drop of water in the sea, or one fiber of Alex Stoner's being, but she wanted him to know that she would be forever changed and changing because of him. Now he would never know. The chance to tell him had gone when he walked out the door. She picked up her paints and turned to leave.

She hesitated. Setting the paint box on a table, she stared at the seascape and felt her heart leap. If they weren't going to be together, she at least had a way to show him she had the guts, if not the heart, to make it on her own. Before she walked out of his house and

into a life without him, she would leave Alex undeniable proof that her boundaries were continuing
to evolve. She worked quickly, and when she was
through, she put down her brush and walked out
onto the patio.

Alex held his breath as the taxi waded through a
herd of goats meandering across the hill road. A loud
sigh of relief whooshed from his lungs when the car
was able to pick up speed again. He had never been
so glad to be on his way to his Zephyros house, or so
anxious. No one had answered the phone when he'd
called from Dimitri's. Instead of allowing himself to
think she'd already left, he tried being positive about
what Sandy's reaction would be when she saw him.
When he talked to her. Explained. Apologized.
Begged her, if he had to, to stay. There was still time,
he told himself, as he spotted the car he'd left for her
in front of the house. Unless Bertram or another
friend had already picked her up.

As the taxi slowed to a stop, Alex dumped several
bills into the front seat and stepped out of the car.
The taxi driver pulled out of the circular driveway
and was headed back into his own cloud of dust
before it had time to settle. Alex was calling her
name as he stepped inside the house. When she
didn't answer, he went directly to his bedroom. Their
bedroom. And then to the guest room she'd used for
the first weeks of her stay. No reason to panic, he
told himself. She had to be around here someplace.
He continued down the hall, opening and slamming
doors as he went.

On the plane ride back to Zephyros he'd practiced what he was going to say to her. He couldn't remember it all now. Hurrying into the kitchen, he tried piecing his speech back together. How did it go? He actually looked forward to Christmas in Atlanta with her. Her folks were terrific people, and he was sorry he'd forgotten to mention that to her. Because of her, he'd called his mother from the airport—she'd cried, and he'd got a frog in his throat. *Sandy, where are you?* He caught his breath as he went into the living room. What else was he going to tell her? He was flexible. Yes, that was it. They could live half the year in the States and the other half in Greece. They could live anywhere she wanted, as long as they were together. He'd been in love with her from the first moment she made him laugh. And he now knew he didn't have to be afraid to act on that love.

Attempting to locate a logical thread in his speech, he tried pushing back the truth now looming over him. He wasn't going to give his speech. *She was gone.* He sank into a chair, loosened his tie, and dropped his head back on the cushion. Then held his breath. Slowly lifting his head, he stared across the room at the seascape on the easel. He blinked twice, then, squinting, stood up and walked over to it.

She'd painted herself into his seascape. Her waist-deep, arms-raised profile gave the appearance of motion, as if she were about to dive into the oncoming wave. Her glistening, creamy-pink figure, rose-tipped breasts, and dark, wet hair contrasted invitingly with the blue water surrounding her. Alex's gaze strayed to the open box of paints and the two brushes stiffening with paint. He picked one up, rolling it between his thumb and forefinger. Why would she leave and not take her paints? And she always gave them a meticulous cleaning after each painting session. It was so unlike Sandy. The brush suddenly stilled between his fingers. She wasn't gone. In one smooth movement he dropped the brush back into the box, then headed for the patio door. He still had a chance.

It was getting late; she had to leave. Pulling her fingers through the water, she looked around the little cove, its sandy beach and its high rock walls. Soon the warmly familiar feeling this place gave her would vanish. Just like Alex. Treading the clear blue water, she allowed herself to sink slowly forward into it. Diving deep, she welcomed the sensation of one final embrace from Alex's private piece of the Aegean. The experience of swimming nude was just as he'd described it. Exhilarating, almost spiritual, a sense of being one with the sea. If only he were here to share it with. Her salty tears mixed with the cool water as she arched her back and pulled herself to the surface.

"I saw the painting."

Planting her feet on the sandy bottom, she whirled around as quickly as the water would allow. "Alex!"

Crouching chin-high in the water several yards from her, he stared at her. Waiting. Lowering his chin and mouth below the water, his blues eyes intensified their focus on her.

She swallowed. "I—I wanted you to know I'd changed. Because of you." She stood a little taller so that the swell of her breasts rose out of the water like shiny pink globes. "And that I'm still changing."

He stared at her until his eyes burned and the lump in his throat eased enough for him to speak. He stood up, then walked closer to her. "Listen, I can't stand this any longer. I love you, Sandy. I love you so much that the thought of you leaving makes me crazy. Tell me what I have to do to make you stay here and marry me."

"Marry you?"

"Yes, marry me. I love you, Sandy. I want you to be my wife, I want us to be a family, to have a family." As he spoke, he watched her eyes widen. "I'll build you a country club with tennis courts and the best golf course in all of Greece." She was nodding and crying and laughing all at the same time. "Yes?" he asked.

"Yes, but only if you don't build that country club. I don't want anything changed on this island except us."

He closed the space between them and began a kiss that ended under water. Seconds later they burst through the surface, gasping for breath through sputtering fits of laughter. He slid his hands along her hips and over her backside. "All summer I tried to get you to skinny-dip, and I almost missed it."

Smoothing her fingers along his lips, she teased him with batting eyelashes. "Well, you would have had the painting."

"The painting," he repeated, drawing her close. She wrapped her legs around his waist. "The painting is perfect, but I have to tell you, I'm enjoying the real thing even more." He kissed her soundly on the lips. "What about you?"

"What about me?"

He lifted her out of the water and looked up into her face. "What do you think about skinny-dipping . . . with me?"

As he tenderly lowered her back in the water, she wrapped her legs around his waist again and ran her finger down his patrician nose. "It's some kind of wonderful," she whispered right before she kissed him.

THE EDITOR'S CORNER

There's no better way to get into the springtime mood than to read the six fabulous LOVESWEPTs coming your way. Humorous and serious, sexy and tender, with heroes and heroines you'll long remember, these novels are guaranteed to turn May into a merry month indeed.

Leading this great lineup is Linda Jenkins with **TALL ORDER**, LOVESWEPT #612. At 6'7", Gray Kincaid is certainly one long, tall hunk, just the kind of man statuesque Garnet Brindisi has been waiting for. And with her flamboyant, feisty manner, she's just the one-woman heat wave who can finally melt the cool reserve of the ex-basketball star called the Iceman. . . . Linda's writing makes the courtship between this unlikely couple a very exciting one to follow.

Please welcome Janis Reams Hudson, bestselling and award-winning author of historical and contemporary romances, and her first LOVESWEPT, **TRUTH OR DARE**, #613. In this touching story, Rachel Fredrick dons a shapeless dress, wig, and glasses, convinced the disguise will forever hide her real identity—and notorious past. She doesn't count on her boss, Jared Morgan, discovering the truth and daring her to let him heal her pain. Enjoy one of New Faces of '93!

STROKE BY STROKE, LOVESWEPT #614 by Patt Bucheister, is how Turner Knight wants to convince Emma Valerian she's the only woman for him. For two years she's been the best paralegal Turner has ever worked with—but the way his body heats up whenever she walks into his office has nothing to do with business. Now she's quitting and Turner can at last confess his hunger and desire. We know you'll treasure this stirring romance from Patt.

In her new LOVESWEPT, Diane Pershing gives you a dangerously sexy hero who offers nothing but **SATISFACTION**, #615. An irresistibly wicked rebel, T. R. is every woman's dream, but Kate O'Brien has vowed never to fall for another heartbreaker. Still, how can she resist a man who warns her she'll be bored with a safe, predictable guy, then dares her to play with his fire? Diane tells this story with breathtaking passion.

Prepare to thrill to romance as you read Linda Warren's second LOVESWEPT, **SWEPT AWAY**, #616. Jake Marlow never intended to return to the family whale-watching business, but he smells sabotage in the air—and he has to consider every possible suspect, including Maria Santos, the exquisitely beautiful fleet manager. The sparks of desire between these two can probably set fire to the ocean! A powerful romance from a powerful storyteller.

Adrienne Staff returns to LOVESWEPT with **PLEASURE IN THE SAND**, #617. In this heart-stirring romance, Jody Conners's nightmare of getting lost at sea turns into a dream when she's rescued by movie star Eric Ransom. Years ago Hollywood's gorgeous bad boy had suddenly dropped out of the public eye, and when he takes Jody to his private island, she discovers only she has the power to coax him—and his guarded heart—out of hiding. Welcome back, Adrienne!

On sale this month from Bantam are three fabulous novels. Teresa Medeiros follows her bestselling **HEATHER**

AND VELVET with **ONCE AN ANGEL**, a captivating historical romance that sweeps from the wilds of an exotic paradise to the elegance of Victorian England. Emily Claire Scarborough sails halfway around the world to find Justin Connor, the man who had cheated her out of her inheritance—and is determined to make him pay with nothing less than his heart.

With **IN A ROGUE'S ARMS**, Virginia Lynn delivers an enchanting, passion-filled retelling of the beloved Robin Hood tale, set in Texas in the 1870s. When Cale Hardin robs Chloe Mitchell's carriage, she swears to take revenge . . . even as she finds herself succumbing to the fascination of this bold and brazen outlaw.

IN A ROGUE'S ARMS is the first book in Bantam's ONCE UPON A TIME romances—passionate historical romances inspired by beloved fairy tales, myths, and legends, penned by some of the finest romance authors writing today, and featuring the most beautiful front and stepback covers. Be sure to look for **PROMISE ME MAGIC** by Patricia Camden, inspired by "Puss in Boots," coming in the summer of 1993, and **CAPTURE THE NIGHT** by Geralyn Dawson, inspired by "Beauty and the Beast," coming in the late fall of 1993.

Favorite LOVESWEPT author Fran Baker makes a spectacular debut in FANFARE with **THE LADY AND THE CHAMP**, which Julie Garwood has already praised as "Unforgettable . . . a warm, wonderful knockout of a book." You'll cheer as Maureen Bryant and Jack Ryan risk anything—even Jack's high-stakes return to the ring—to fight for their chance at love.

Bantam/Doubleday/Dell welcomes Jane Feather with the Doubleday hardcover edition of **VIRTUE**. Set in Regency England, this highly sensual tale brings together a strong-willed beauty who makes her living at the gaming tables and the arrogant nobleman determined to best her with passion.

Happy reading!

With warmest wishes,

Nita Taublib
Associate Publisher
LOVESWEPT and FANFARE

OFFICIAL RULES TO WINNERS CLASSIC SWEEPSTAKES

No Purchase necessary. To enter the sweepstakes follow instructions found elsewhere in this offer. You can also enter the sweepstakes by hand printing your name, address, city, state and zip code on a 3" x 5" piece of paper and mailing it to: Winners Classic Sweepstakes, P.O. Box 785, Gibbstown, NJ 08027. Mail each entry separately. Sweepstakes begins 12/1/91. Entries must be received by 6/1/93. Some presentations of this sweepstakes may feature a deadline for the Early Bird prize. If the offer you receive does, then to be eligible for the Early Bird prize your entry must be received according to the Early Bird date specified. Not responsible for lost, late, damaged, misdirected, illegible or postage due mail. Mechanically reproduced entries are not eligible. All entries become property of the sponsor and will not be returned.

Prize Selection/Validations: Winners will be selected in random drawings on or about 7/30/93, by VENTURA ASSOCIATES, INC., an independent judging organization whose decisions are final. Odds of winning are determined by total number of entries received. Circulation of this sweepstakes is estimated not to exceed 200 million. Entrants need not be present to win. All prizes are guaranteed to be awarded and delivered to winners. Winners will be notified by mail and may be required to complete an affidavit of eligibility and release of liability which must be returned within 14 days of date of notification or alternate winners will be selected. Any guest of a trip winner will also be required to execute a release of liability. Any prize notification letter or any prize returned to a participating sponsor, Bantam Doubleday Dell Publishing Group, Inc., its participating divisions or subsidiaries, or VENTURA ASSOCIATES, INC. as undeliverable will be awarded to an alternate winner. Prizes are not transferable. No multiple prize winners except as may be necessary due to unavailability, in which case a prize of equal or greater value will be awarded. Prizes will be awarded approximately 90 days after the drawing. All taxes, automobile license and registration fees, if applicable, are the sole responsibility of the winners. Entry constitutes permission (except where prohibited) to use winners' names and likenesses for publicity purposes without further or other compensation.

Participation: This sweepstakes is open to residents of the United States and Canada, except for the province of Quebec. This sweepstakes is sponsored by Bantam Doubleday Dell Publishing Group, Inc. (BDD), 666 Fifth Avenue, New York, NY 10103. Versions of this sweepstakes with different graphics will be offered in conjunction with various solicitations or promotions by different subsidiaries and divisions of BDD. Employees and their families of BDD, its division, subsidiaries, advertising agencies, and VENTURA ASSOCIATES, INC., are not eligible.

Canadian residents, in order to win, must first correctly answer a time limited arithmetical skill testing question. Void in Quebec and wherever prohibited or restricted by law. Subject to all federal, state, local and provincial laws and regulations.

Prizes: The following values for prizes are determined by the manufacturers' suggested retail prices or by what these items are currently known to be selling for at the time this offer was published. Approximate retail values include handling and delivery of prizes. Estimated maximum retail value of prizes: 1 Grand Prize ($27,500 if merchandise or $25,000 Cash); 1 First Prize ($3,000); 5 Second Prizes ($400 each); 35 Third Prizes ($100 each); 1,000 Fourth Prizes ($9.00 each) ; 1 Early Bird Prize ($5,000); Total approximate maximum retail value is $50,000. Winners will have the option o selecting any prize offered at level won. Automobile winner must have a valid driver's license at the time the car is awarded. Trips are subject to space and departure availability. Certain black-out dates may apply. Travel must be completed within one year from the time the prize is awarded. Minors mus be accompanied by an adult. Prizes won by minors will be awarded in the name of parent or lega guardian.

For a list of Major Prize Winners (available after 7/30/93): send a self-addressed, stampe envelope entirely separate from your entry to: Winners Classic Sweepstakes Winners, P.O. Box 825 Gibbstown, NJ 08027. Requests must be received by 6/1/93. DO NOT SEND ANY OTHE CORRESPONDENCE TO THIS P.O. BOX.